TOO CLOSE

(A Morgan Stark FBI Suspense Thriller—Book 2)

Rylie Dark

Rylie Dark

Bestselling author Rylie Dark is author of the SADIE PRICE FBI SUSPENSE THRILLER series, comprising six books (and counting); the MIA NORTH FBI SUSPENSE THRILLER series, comprising six books (and counting); the CARLY SEE FBI SUSPENSE THRILLER, comprising six books (and counting); and the MORGAN STARK FBI SUSPENSE THRILLER, comprising three books (and counting).

An avid reader and lifelong fan of the mystery and thriller genres, Rylie loves to hear from you, so please feel free to visit www.ryliedark.com to learn more and stay in touch.

ISBN: 978-1-0943-9565-4

PROLOGUE

The cute bartender with the earring yelled out that it was last call.

Angelica smiled down at her phone. This app was the absolute bomb and this guy on the screen seemed like a real possibility. His online flirting game was on point and his photo looked better than average. At least he wasn't holding a fish. What was with that anyway? Did men think women wanted proof of their ability to provide food in the form of fish?

Of course, all that good stuff about this dude could be a lie. You never know who you are really talking with on an app until you meet in real life.

And that was going to happen soon. This weekend. A pleasant little shiver of anticipation ran through her. It had been a while since she'd been willing to meet someone and this felt right. She'd actually offered to meet him for a drink right then and there, even told him what bar she was at. He couldn't make it, though.

She sent a last message and gathered her purse and keys. Time to go home.

She stepped out of the bar, a tiny bit unsteady on the heels she wore. Not entirely practical, but she knew they made her calves pop. She wanted to look good when she went out. She still hadn't ruled out meeting somebody the old-fashioned way, like at a party or a bar, but she dreaded the idea of having The Talk with a new romantic interest.

Not having to have The Talk was definitely a selling point for the app. What a relief to have that out of the way before she even had coffee with someone.

Out on the street, the night was still muggy. She lifted her hair off her neck to cool off, but there wasn't any breeze. She was alone on the street and it was dark. No one would see her, would see what she was doing her best to keep hidden from the world. She decided to chance it and unwound the scarf she was wearing around her neck. Lord. Every summer, the humidity and heat in DC surprised her.

Swaying a bit, she made her way down the sidewalk to the lot where she'd parked her car. When she'd arrived, the place had been jumping. It had seemed worth it to pay a little extra for the unmanned lot rather than driving around in circles hoping a space would open up

1

on the street.

Now she wasn't so sure. The lot wasn't nearly as well-lit as the street and her little coupe sat tucked into a back corner. She paused for a second. Peering into the gloom, she felt a little prickle of unease at the back of her neck, as if someone was watching her.

She shook herself. She was being ridiculous. Or, at least, paranoid. Keeping her phone in her hand to light her way, she tottered across the gravel to her car.

"Dammit!" Broken glass sparkled in the light of her flashlight app. Somebody had broken the back window of her car. Smashed it, in fact. Why? She hadn't left anything worth stealing in there. She knew better than that. She'd better call the cops to make a report so her insurance would cover at least part of the damage. Stupid thieves. It's not like the cops would do anything. Maybe she could go home and call it in from there. The lot was giving her major creeps.

"Excuse me," said a man's voice behind her.

Angelica, hand pressed to her chest, turned to see a man sitting on the bumper of a truck parked across the row from her. Where did he come from? He wasn't there when she walked up. No one was. She was sure. She hadn't been so distracted from her busted rear window that she would have missed an entire person. Had he been hiding? She swallowed hard, pushing down the panicked feeling that was rising up inside of her. Something wasn't right about this guy. Something wasn't right about this situation. "You startled me."

"Give me your phone." He stood and walked toward her. Was that a baseball bat by his side? Could he have been the one to bash in her back window? She looked from him to her car and back at him.

Angelica didn't know what this guy's game was, but she wasn't going to stand around to find out. Heart pounding, she whirled and ran toward the sidewalk, but her stupid heel caught in one of the ruts in the lot and her ankle rolled. She caught her balance, but it was too late.

The man grabbed her arm and whirled her around, snatching the phone out of her hand.

A whimper escaped her as she struggled against his grip. He was too strong. She couldn't get away. She screamed, but the street was deserted. There was no one nearby to hear her.

Holding the phone and the bat in his right hand, he used his thumb to scroll through the phone. A sharp intake of breath. "Is that how you did it?" he whispered. "That's how you cheated?"

"What are you talking about? Cheated on who?" Who was this guy? She pulled hard against him, bracing her feet against the ground.

"You're hurting me. Let me go."

The man abruptly let go of her arm, sending her windmilling backwards. Then he dropped her phone to the ground and smashed it with the bat, hitting it over and over.

Angelica caught her balance. Her keys were still in her hand. Maybe she could get to her car while he was busy turning her phone into electronic dust. She ducked around him and made a run for it.

"Where the hell do you think you're going, you little slut?"

She glanced over her shoulder. He'd finished pounding her phone. He pointed the bat at her and advanced. She stumbled again, but made it to the car, nearly in tears from the fear. She swore to herself that she was never going to wear heels again. Please, just let her get home.

"I don't know what you're talking about. You've got me confused with someone else." She hit the button to unlock the car doors and grabbed the door. "I've never even met you. How could I have cheated on you?"

He hit the ground with the baseball bat, and gravel flew in all directions. There was a sharp sting on her calf as one of the pieces hit her. "Shut up," he growled.

She got the door open and slid in. All she had to do was get the door shut and hit the start button. Her hands shook as she stabbed at the button. "Come on. Come on," she pleaded, not even sure to whom. She pulled at the door, but he already stood in the way.

"You're not getting away that easy," he said.

Then he grabbed her by the hair and pulled her out of the car.

CHAPTER ONE

"Dr. Stark," said Dr. Preston Kane, his voice loud in the hushed hospital auditorium. "Dr. Stark!"

Morgan startled. "Yes. Sorry. Could you repeat the question?"

Kane scowled at him, his eyebrows coming together in a V. He was a white man in his sixties. Distinguished. A touch of silver at his temples, but reasonably fit. He'd worked at Georgetown for over thirty years and probably would refuse to retire for another twenty at least. He was officious, condescending, and, as luck would have it, in charge of the hearing deciding what disciplinary action the hospital would take against Morgan. "I asked you if you could describe for the panel what you did on the night in question?"

Morgan sighed. He'd have been happy to stipulate all these details, but Kane clearly wanted to add a little slice of humiliation to the shit sandwich he was making Morgan eat. "I returned to the hospital and searched for patients who had been treated by Lexa Windham and who had had their labs run by Michelle Schultz. I then reported those findings to Special Agent Danielle Hernandez."

"Were you aware that you were violating HIPAA regulations by doing so?" Kane asked.

"Yes." Morgan leaned back in his chair.

Kane stared at him, clearly expecting Morgan to offer some kind of defense for what he'd done.

Morgan had no intention of doing so. As far as he was concerned, everything he'd done had been worth it. What he'd discovered by bending the rules here and there had led to them stopping a deranged serial killer who would have killed again and again and again. Hesitating for a few more hours would have left at least one more victim dead. Who knew how much longer it would have taken to catch the culprit?

He only wished he'd been able to do it sooner. He looked down, a wave of sadness crashing over him. Lives were lost unnecessarily. Promising lives. Innocent lives. His only satisfaction was that the man responsible would be spending the rest of his life in prison, unable to ever hurt anyone again. He stood by his actions.

"Dr. Stark!" Dr. Kane raised his voice again. "Are you listening?"

Once again, Morgan forced himself to focus on the proceedings. He should care. He should care a lot. He just couldn't seem to.

The career that he'd dedicated his life to, that he may well have sacrificed his marriage for, hung in the balance and he couldn't bring himself to do much beyond go through the motions. He looked out over the spectators in the auditorium.

Normally, the auditorium was set up for presentations and Morbidity and Mortality conferences with all the chairs and tables facing the front of the room. It still largely was, except Kane had insisted that Morgan be seated facing the assembled audience of his peers as if he was on trial, which he supposed he was, in a way.

More people attended the hearing than Morgan had expected. There were a few out there with gleams in their eyes, looking for a little schadenfreude. Morgan hadn't always been as careful as he could have been about trampling the egos of his peers. It wasn't so much that he didn't suffer fools gladly, he just didn't suffer them at all. He'd stepped on some toes and bruised some egos, never only for the joy of it, but always in service of a patient's well-being. Apparently, it mattered more to him than it did to others, some of whom were here today to watch Morgan get taken down a peg. Well, let them.

One friendly face stood out in the crowd. Ashley. She looked understated and professional in a dark navy suit with a narrow pinstripe running through it, a single string of pearls around her neck, and blonde hair neatly styled. Even though he'd signed the papers and their divorce was proceeding, he still thought of her as his wife. Maybe he always would. He wished he didn't feel so responsible for the worry lines on her forehead. There'd been a time when he could have smoothed those away with a touch.

"Is there anything else you'd like to add, Dr. Stark?" Kane asked, wrapping up the hearing.

Morgan shook his head. "Not at this time. No."

"The board will now confer." Kane gestured with a head nod toward the rest of the panel. The group of four men and three women filed out.

Morgan stood, legs stiff from sitting for so long. After months of drinking too much, eating nothing but take-out and cafeteria food, and sitting around feeling sorry for himself, he'd started running again. His muscles creaked, but in a good way now. He felt stronger and clearer. He made his way to Ashley.

She moved aside her briefcase that had been on the seat next to her

5

to allow him to sit down.

"How do you think it went?" He slumped into the seat, hitching up the legs of his gray trousers.

Around them, people began to file out of the auditorium. The show was over. Morgan ignored the surreptitious glances being cast his way. He didn't care what other people thought. He never had. He wasn't going to start now.

Ashley took in a deep breath and let it out slowly. "Morgan, do you even want to keep practicing medicine?" A true daughter of the South, her honeyed drawl combined with her blonde hair and big blue eyes had fooled a few people into thinking she wasn't too bright. Most of them had paid for that assumption. Ashley was sharp as a tack, insightful, and incisive.

He straightened. "Of course!" Was he being honest with himself, though? He wasn't sure. He'd spent so much of his life getting to this point. Would he really give it up? Forever? "I at least want the option."

"It didn't really look like it up there." She stood up, brushing the wrinkles out of the front of her skirt. "Come on. I'll buy you a cup of coffee. They probably won't make a decision for at least a few days."

He'd rather have a beer, but coffee would have to do. "Sure," he said. "It's not like I have anything else on my schedule."

Ashley extended her hand to him, he took it and stood. It felt good to touch her, even if it was in this limited platonic way. Sometimes the amount he missed her nearly took his knees out from under him.

The auditorium was almost empty now. They made their way up toward the exit doors, their footsteps barely making a whisper on the carpeted stairs. They hadn't even made it to the top row when Morgan's cell phone buzzed.

He pulled it from his pocket and stared at it for a moment, not quite certain he could believe what he was seeing.

"What is it?" Ashely asked.

"They made a decision."

"That was fast."

Morgan made a face. Fast was an understatement. They'd barely had time to get to the conference room, much less spend time conferring. The hearing had been for show. The board had clearly already made its decision before he'd answered a single question.

"Well?" Ashley asked, her hands twisted in front of her. "What did they say?"

He sighed. "I'm being suspended without pay for the next six months."

Ashley looked down at her feet. "We expected as much. That's not so bad."

His heart swelled at her use of "we." There was still a connection there for him. He suspected Ashely felt it too. As for the matter at hand, though, she was right. They had expected the suspension. The Board had to do something about Morgan's breach of patient privacy. It would be a terrible precedent to set if they didn't. He'd hoped it wouldn't be for more than a few weeks, though. Apparently, they wanted to send a more significant message than that.

"So at the end of six months, you can come back." Ashley gave him a weak smile. "It'll go by quickly. You'll see."

He wasn't so sure about that. "They're reserving the right to further review."

Ashley sucked in a breath.

That wasn't great news. It meant they could still decide to terminate him completely.

Ashley slid her arm through his. "Come on. How about we make that coffee a martini instead?"

He laughed. "Sounds like a plan." He pulled her arm in close to his side, enjoying the feel of her soft warmth against him, and they made their way out the doors of the auditorium.

They'd barely made it into the wide hallway when a familiar figure strode toward them. Tall and leggy, dark hair pulled back into a low ponytail, and wearing a black pantsuit, Special Agent Danielle Hernandez walked across the space with purpose and determination. What was she doing here? Had she somehow already been informed of the Board's decision?

"Dr. Stark," she said, then turned to Ashley. "Ms. Stark."

"Ashley, please."

The two women shook hands. They'd met before during the wrap up of a case Morgan had worked with Danielle on before. From what Morgan could tell, they'd sized each other up quickly, according each other the respect of two women who knew what it was like to succeed in male-dominated fields. "Good to see you again," Danielle said and then turned her attention back to Morgan. "How'd the hearing go?" she asked.

So she had been keeping track of him. "Could be worse." He didn't feel like going over the details right then. "What brings you here?"

She tilted her head to one side and looked up at him. "Still interested in being an FBI consultant?"

His heart sped up. Working with Danielle on the Georgetown

Hospital murders case had been a life saver for him. Sure, it had gotten him suspended just now, but at least he was really living and not going through the motions the way he had been for months. It had been a good deal of what had shocked him out of the soul-sucking depression he'd been sliding into. Besides, what else did he have to do for the next six months? He certainly wasn't going to be practicing medicine. "Yes. I'm absolutely interested."

"Great," she said, turning to walk toward the door, assuming he would follow. "Come on. We've got a case."

CHAPTER TWO

Morgan followed Danielle out of the hospital to where her SUV was parked. The humidity hit him like a solid wall of damp air. Both of them removed their suit jackets immediately and Danielle blasted the black SUV's air conditioner at peak capacity. It barely made a dent.

"Do you want to talk about it?" Danielle asked him as she steered them through DC traffic.

"Not especially." Morgan looked down at his hands. He needed time to think about the Board's decision and his feelings about it. "Want to tell me about this case?"

"Not especially." Danielle flashed him a grin, and then shook her head. "I'd rather have you come at it fresh without any preconceptions."

"Okay, then. How about them Nats?" he asked.

Danielle snorted. "I don't think either of us are very adept at small talk."

"True that." The silence was companionable, easy. His heart rate, however, increased with anticipation as they neared the FBI building. These days, running and the thought of helping investigate cases for the FBI seemed to be the only things that could do that. He'd barely broken a sweat during that morning's hearing on the fate of his professional life, but his hands got clammy as he walked with Danielle through the lobby of the FBI building, nearly bouncing on his toes as they went.

"Morning, Agent Hernandez. Nice to see you again, Dr. Stark," Marilynn Roderick, the security guard, said as she produced a Visitor's badge for Morgan and waved them both through. She'd been a whole lot less friendly the first time Morgan had tried to get through that turnstile. Now he was at least a semi-familiar face and he knew that Marilynn would be 100 percent behind anything that Danielle wanted.

"We'll need to get you a permanent one of those," Danielle said, indicating his badge as she pushed the button for the elevator.

A grin twitched at the edge of Morgan's lips that he stilled, his excitement at being a more permanent part of Danielle's team was countered by his awareness that someone must have lost their life for him to be called in. The sensation was familiar. It had been what he'd felt for most of his life in medicine. He loved what he did. Nailing a difficult diagnosis had been challenging and exciting, but for it to get to him meant that someone had been suffering and usually for some time. He loved solving the intellectual puzzle but tried to always keep in mind that it was a means to an end. The point was to help someone, not to entertain himself.

They got off on the fifth floor and Morgan matched his stride with Danielle's as they walked down the hall. She waved her badge in front of the RFID reader and they entered the bullpen. Several agents looked up as they went through. Danielle acknowledged them with a nod or a wave. Morgan could feel their gazes on his back as they continued through.

"Is there something stuck to my shoe?" he leaned down to ask Danielle in a quiet voice.

She shot him a questioning look.

"If looks were lasers, I'd have more than a few holes in my back."

"They're probably wondering what you're doing here." Danielle continued down the hall without a backwards glance.

Morgan wondered too, but he knew Danielle wouldn't have asked him to consult if she hadn't had a reason. Danielle went past the room they'd used before. "We're in the big conference room this time," she explained, pushing open a door at the end of the hall.

Not only was the room bigger than the one they'd used to track the killer they'd caught only a few weeks ago, it also had more people in it. Two agents — a Black woman and a white man — tacked photos onto two whiteboards, adding notes beside them.

"Henry, Divinia," Danielle said. "I'd like you to meet Dr. Morgan Stark. He'll be working as a consultant on this case with us."

Morgan shook both their hands.

"Heard about what you did on the Georgetown Hospital murders case," Divinia said. "Pleasure to be working with you, sir."

Her handshake was firm. She wore her straightened hair pulled back into a bun. Her black pantsuit looked like an exact replica of Danielle's.

"Sir," Henry also shook Morgan's hand. "Looking forward to hearing what you have to say about this new case."

Henry's suit was charcoal gray and single-breasted with a pinstripe. His blond hair was cut in a crew cut fade. He had that preppy look that could have easily gotten him cast as the bad guy in a teen movie from the eighties.

"Good to meet you both," Morgan said.

10

Danielle gestured for him to sit down at the table in the center of the room. "Show us what you've got," she said.

The two younger agents exchanged a glance and then Divinia stood next to the whiteboard on the left.

"Our first victim is Kimberly Samson." Divinia gestured up at a photo of a smiling young woman with blonde hair cut in a short spiky style that accentuated her high cheekbones and large blue eyes. She reminded Morgan a little of Ashley. "Thirty-two-year-old white female living alone in a small rental house in Ivy City. Single. Worked as a marketing manager for Astute Insurance."

Divinia tapped a pushpin that had been put into the Ivy City neighborhood on a map that was on the whiteboard. Then she pulled another set of photos out of a folder and tacked them to the board. "On Sunday night of last week, someone bashed in a back window and entered the home. It appears that Kimberly was running for her cell phone that she'd left charging in her bedroom when her assailant caught up to her."

Morgan was used to blood and gore. It was part of being a doctor, but he physically recoiled at what he saw in the crime scene photos once Divinia backed away. Someone had beaten the woman beyond recognition. The contrast between the smiling photo at the top of the board and what was left of Kimberly Samson was jarring. The fact that she had resembled Ashley in life made his stomach turn.

"Cause of death will likely be blunt force trauma. The body was discovered by a friend from work who was concerned when Ms. Samson didn't show up for an important meeting and wasn't answering her phone. Nothing of value was taken from the home, including the eighty dollars found in the victim's wallet." Divinia paused to tack up a few more photos showing a big screen television set and a computer. "Her cell phone, however, was destroyed."

Another photo went up. This one of a phone that had been smashed to bits. Divinia sat down and Henry stood.

"Our second victim was Angelica McNally." Henry pointed to the second whiteboard, where a photo of another white woman smiled down at them. This one had long brown hair. While both women were white, there wasn't a lot of resemblance between them. "Ms. McNally, a twenty-eight-year-old white woman, was attacked last night in a parking lot in the H Street Corridor." He tapped the second pushpin on the map. "She was an administrative assistant at a consulting firm."

This time, Morgan had braced himself for the crime scene photos. They were every bit as brutal as the ones of Kimberly Samson, but he

11

didn't flinch outwardly. Inwardly, he was repulsed. How could one human being do this to another? Kimberly lay sprawled across a gravel lot, bloodied and broken, the contents of her purse scattered around her.

Henry tapped a small square in one photo. "Her wallet was recovered at the scene. It had forty-two dollars in it. As far as we can tell, nothing was taken from the wallet or from her vehicle, which was parked nearby with its driver's side door open." Henry pulled another photo from his folder. "Her cell phone was also smashed."

Morgan stood up and walked to the whiteboards to get a better look at the photos. He shook his head at the wreckage of these two bodies. How angry would you have to be to do that to another human being? For a second, he imagined what each of those women must have gone through in the last minutes of their lives. The pain. The fear. He grabbed onto the back of a chair to steady himself.

Still, why was he here? Neither woman's name nor profile photo rang a bell with him. Neither were healthcare workers. There wasn't any obvious connection to him.

"Was there blood or tissue from anyone else at the scenes?" he asked. Maybe the medical link had to do with the perpetrator, the unsub as Danielle would undoubtedly call him. Maybe they'd found something in evidence left at the scene that he could help them interpret.

"Not at Ms. Samson's," Divinia said. "The forensic unit is still processing the other scene. With it being a public parking lot, there's likely going to be a number of other samples, but we won't know if any of them could belong to the perpetrator. At least not until we have a suspect to match them to."

So that wasn't it. Morgan stepped closer to the photographs. Someone had gone much further than necessary to kill here. There was rage behind what had been done to these two women. Their faces were nearly obliterated. It was personal.

"Any connection between the two women?" he asked.

"Not that we've found as of yet," Henry said, walking over to stand next to Morgan. "We're still looking, though. Right now, we're waiting on a subpoena for their phone and email records. If necessary, we'll get a warrant. I'm hoping their providers will cooperate, given the circumstances."

"What's with the map?" Morgan frowned at the two pushpins, trying to figure out what significance they might have.

Henry leaned back against the table, arms crossed over his chest. "We're trying to get a handle on where he's striking geographically. If we can figure out his comfort zone, it might give us some clues as to where he lives or works. He'll have wanted to strike in an area that he's familiar with, so he knows where and when to kill and how to get away without witnesses, but he won't want it to be too close to his home or work. It's another pattern to examine that might bear fruit."

Interesting. There was so much to learn about how to look at a crime or at a criminal. Maybe that was what he liked. A new frontier to challenge him. Morgan stepped even closer to the photos, turning off his emotions, blocking out his natural inclination to empathy. It would only get in the way at the moment. He had to step back, as he would if he was trying to make a diagnosis at the hospital. He went back and forth between the two women. Both had some kind of discoloration around their collarbones. At first, he thought it was a shadow on Kimberly Samson, but it was too big a coincidence for both of them to have the exact same shadow.

"What is that on their chests?" he asked, pointing to the area he was looking at.

Danielle looked over at Henry with her eyebrows raised. He held his hands in front of himself and took a couple of steps back.

"What?" Morgan asked. Some kind of silent communication had happened there that had to do with him, he suspected.

Danielle stepped up and stood next to him. "It's why I called you in. Both women have a similar kind of rash on their chests. It's the only connection we've found between the two of them beyond the similarity in the MOs. If the connection between them is something medical, well, I couldn't think of a better person to call in to help us sort it out."

Morgan glanced over at Henry, whose face was studiously blank. He'd hazard a guess that Henry hadn't been too keen on having Morgan called in and had questioned his superior officer about it. Feeling like he'd just passed some test that he hadn't known he was taking, Morgan turned to Danielle. "I'd like to see the bodies in person."

"I'm not sure what good that would do." She turned away from the photos. "There's not a lot recognizable left of them."

"I know, but if there is something else, some other small detail that might help, I'm not going to get it from looking at these photos. I need to see them and examine them in person." He didn't remind her that it was a small detail that only he had noticed on a victim's body that had been the first step in unraveling their previous case. A scraped knee. That had been the one little detail that no one else had thought was important that had started them on the path of finding a murderer. From the pensive look on Danielle's face, he didn't have to remind her of that.

She nodded. "I'll make a call."

CHAPTER THREE

This trip to the Medical Examiner's office was significantly different than the last time Morgan had been there. Last time, he had to bully and cajole his way into seeing the body of a murder victim. It went a lot more smoothly with an FBI escort. All it required was a flash of Danielle's badge. Morgan was relieved that there was a different security guard at the desk. It hadn't been his finest moment when he'd threatened to report the man to his superiors. In Morgan's defense, he'd been nearly wild with grief at the time, desperate to do something — anything — to find the person who had killed one of the most promising residents he'd ever seen, one who'd reminded him all too much of his sister Fiona. Just the thought of her name brought a little ache to his chest. It had been more than a decade since his sister had disappeared without a trace, but he still missed her.

For this visit to the OCME, the Office of the Chief Medical Examiner, both he and Danielle were expected. After a check of their IDs, they were ushered to the elevator bank. He was truly part of this process now, not an interloper with an agenda of his own. The thought had him standing a little straighter and taller.

Dr. Morris, the Medical Examiner, hadn't forgotten him, though.

Still in a rumpled suit, Morris met Danielle and Morgan as they got off the elevator on the fifth floor. He had a neatly trimmed beard, a pair of tortoiseshell glasses and wore his hair in a close-cut afro.

"Agent Hernandez." He nodded to Danielle. "Nice to see you again, Dr. Stark."

Morgan doubted that was true, but he wasn't going to argue. The man had been kinder to Morgan than he'd had expected on his last visit, and it seemed that behavior was going to continue.

Morris beckoned for them to follow him down the hallway.

"What can you tell us so far?" Danielle asked.

Morris glanced over his shoulder at her. "Not much yet. We won't be doing the full autopsy on either woman for another day."

The backlog at the DC ME's office had been notorious at one point. Morris had done a lot toward clearing that up, but the nation's capital was still a busy and sometimes violent town. Morgan was glad they'd gotten there before the procedure was performed, though. He wanted to see the bodies as they were.

Morris led them into the body storage room, consulted a clipboard hanging on the wall, and pulled out one of the drawers.

He paused. "You're both prepared? Ms. Samson and Ms. McNally were quite brutally beaten."

"We're aware," Danielle assured him. "We've seen photos, but Dr. Stark felt he should see the bodies in person."

Morris only nodded and pulled down the sheet. A shudder ran through Danielle. Morgan glanced at her to make sure she was all right. The shudder had been momentary. He understood why it had happened, though. It was hard not to react to the ruin that had once been a face that had smiled and frowned, laughed and cried. The photographs had been bad enough. The three-dimensional reality was a hundred times worse.

Morgan nodded at Morris who rolled down more of the sheet. There was bruising around Samson's forearms as if she'd thrown her arms up to protect herself, but also to her ribs and abdomen. Morgan leaned forward to look at the size and shape of the bruising. He looked up at Morris. "Any preliminary thoughts on what made these marks?"

"I can't say for sure, but it seems like the class characteristics would be consistent with a baseball bat." Morris shook his head. "We see those injuries all too often here."

Morgan straightened. "A high percentage of deaths by blunt force trauma are perpetrated with baseball bats."

"I'll want to do more measurements and examinations before I say that conclusively," Morris said.

"Of course," Morgan said.

"The class what now?" Danielle asked, her face still a little pale.

Morris turned to Danielle. "Often times when we see bruises of a consistent size and shape or other points of identification, we can indicate a group of potential weapons. We call those signs class characteristics. In this case, as I said, probably a baseball bat."

Her eyes widened a little. "Anything there that might allow us to narrow that down a bit? There are a lot of kinds of bats. It would be helpful if there was something unique about this one."

Morgan crouched down to view the wounds from a different vantage point. "Probably a wooden bat, not aluminum." He frowned. Something glinted. "Is that glass?"

Morris put on gloves and extracted a fragment from the wound with a pair of tweezers and then held it to the light. "Seems to be." He

16

dropped the shard into a plastic evidence bag and made a notation on it.

Morgan turned to Danielle. "Divinia mentioned the back window of the house had been smashed. I'd guess the attacker used the same instrument to break the window and then to beat Ms. Samson."

"Does this help us at all?" Danielle asked.

Morris pulled the sheet back up over Kimberly Swanson's face. "It could. If you find the actual weapon. There's likely to still be glass embedded in it. It would be awfully difficult to completely clean it. Since it's wood, it will be even more difficult to get all traces of blood and other biological matter off it."

Morgan turned to Danielle. "What about blood spatter analysis at the scene? Do you have someone on that? Cast-off spatter from the weapon would hit the ceiling, walls, furniture. That might give us a bit more information too."

Danielle jotted something in her notebook.

Morgan stood back up. "Any determination on the cause of death?"

Morris shook his head. "No. Although I would put my money on brain injury. I'm sure, based on the violence of the attack, that there will be damage to internal organs, but I can't imagine that she would have succumbed to that before the fractures to her head and neck."

"Again, that fits statistically, especially given the fracture patterns to the mid- and upper-facial bones." Morgan frowned and turned back to Danielle. "Divinia said that Ms. Samson had tried to run. Henry said the same thing about Ms. McNally. Do I have that right?"

She nodded. "Is that significant?"

"For the damage to those mid- and upper- facial bones to have occurred, the murderer had to be facing them. That was a deliberate choice. He must have turned them. He wanted to see their faces as he obliterated them. Even more, he wanted them to see his face as he killed them." Morgan shuddered. The rage behind these killings had been clear to him already. This was personal and focused too. Whoever did this wasn't just angry, he was angry at these particular women. Yet no connection between them had been found. They had to have something in common that triggered this murderer. But what?

"You keep saying he. Any chance we could be looking for a she?" Danielle asked.

"I doubt it." Morgan looked over at Morris. "How tall is Ms. Samson?"

Morris consulted his clipboard. "Around five foot seven."

Morgan turned back to the body. He snapped on a pair of gloves from the box on the tray next to the gurney and brushed back her hair.

17

"Look at the angle of these injuries. He was swinging down from a greater height, right to left. He was enough taller than her that he was able to do that with a great deal of power behind the swing. It's not impossible that it's a woman, but she'd be noticeably tall and very strong."

Because her facial bones were fractured, Ms. Samson's eyes were not quite all the way closed. Because he'd moved her hair back, he could now see a bit more of them. "Does her sclera look yellow to you?"

Morris leaned in as well. "A little."

"Be sure to check bilirubin levels, will you?" It was a small detail, but it stuck out to him as unexpected. Those were exactly the kinds of details he'd use to make a diagnosis. They could mean something here too.

"Absolutely." Morris jotted down a note.

"What might that mean?" Danielle asked.

Morgan blew out a breath. "I'm not sure, but it's odd that a woman this well-nourished would be jaundiced."

He examined the rash on her chest. Up close, he could see that it was almost more of a chain of nodules, raised and red. It spread down her chest toward her abdomen. He'd do some research on rashes when he got a moment.

"Did you want to see Ms. McNally as well?" Morris asked.

Morgan stepped back to allow Morris to roll Ms. Samson back into the drawer. "Of course."

Again, Morris consulted his clipboard and went to a different drawer. He rolled out Ms. McNally and rolled the sheet down. "Same kind of injuries. Same kind of bruises. I'd be very surprised if they weren't made with the same kind of weapon."

Morgan squinted, again seeing a small glint. "Glass in her injuries as well. That could be transfer from the glass that got embedded in the bat when he broke into Samson's home."

Danielle lifted one eyebrow. "Please be sure to compare those samples," she said to the ME. "We'll want to be sure of that. It could be a big point in convincing a jury that these deaths are linked."

Morgan rubbed at his jaw. "But how? That's what I'm not getting."

"It's early days yet," Danielle said. "We'll find it."

Morgan wished he had her confidence. Again he moved to see the body from a different angle, examining the rash. The same large raised red areas were on her chest and abdomen. "What's that on her neck?" he pointed his still gloved hand toward a small lump just above

18

McNally's clavicle.

"Where?" Morris asked.

"Right there." Morgan came around the gurney. He wasn't imagining it. There was some kind of small lump there. "Could I see Ms. Samson again please?"

Morris nodded and glided out the gurney from behind its stainless steel door and pulled the sheet back.

Morgan hadn't noticed it on Samson. It was partly obscured by a particularly nasty bruise, but there was a small lump on her neck as well. "We'll want information on both of those too, please. Might as well run bilirubin levels on Samson as well as McNally."

Morgan shut his eyes for a second, trying to come up with something that would connect the rash, the lumps on the women's necks, and jaundice. Nothing leapt to mind.

Morris wheeled both bodies back in, looking a little queasy. His job wasn't an easy one. Maybe it was getting to him.

"These are tough ones," Morgan said. "It's hard to believe how brutal human beings can be to each other."

Morris pressed his lips together. "It's not that. I'm, for better or worse, used to that. I've seen way too much of it here. It's that I'm not so sure I would have noticed those lumps. We could have gone right past them. The possibility of missing something like that is concerning. I'm pretty sure we would have caught jaundice when we tested the blood, but I'm not certain of that either."

"They're probably nothing," Morgan assured him, although he wasn't sure that was true. "Little lipomas like I suspect that one of being are rarely fatal." Not fatal. No. But important? That he wasn't so sure of. If these medical details were the point of connection between the two women, those lumps could be very important. He snapped his gloves off. Still, odd that both women would have them in similar spots. There was something there. He was sure of it. He just wasn't sure what it was.

"Finished here?" Danielle asked, glancing at her watch.

He nodded. "For now? Where next?"

"I haven't been to the crime scene for Ms. McNally yet and the police are anxious to release the scene."

"What are we waiting for then?" he asked.

CHAPTER FOUR

Danielle pulled into traffic and glanced surreptitiously over her sunglasses at Morgan as he buckled himself in.

What a piece of luck that she'd stumbled on him. Disciplined. Focused. And so damn observant. Sometimes maybe a little too observant. He certainly hadn't missed the exchange between her and Henry.

Henry hadn't been thrilled when she'd said she wanted to bring Morgan in as a consultant. He'd argued that he and Divinia were plenty observant and didn't think bringing a civilian in would be all that helpful.

It was Danielle's team, though. Not Henry's. Although he was clearly gunning for that position. He'd get there. He was smart, capable, driven, but he was also green.

No. This was Danielle's team and there were a lot of eyes watching how she'd run it. Solving the Georgetown Hospital murders had brought her the attention of a lot of people, specifically people in the position of handing out assignments and promotions. For that case, it had been pretty much just her and Morgan. When the Washington DC police had notified the Bureau about these two murders, wondering if they could be connected, she'd been assigned to the case and asked who she'd like working under her.

That had never happened before and she liked it. Being given the opportunity to assemble and lead a team was a huge step up the ladder for her, and she intended to make the most of it.

She was well aware of the contributions Morgan had made to that first case they'd worked together, the one that had led to this opportunity. While she hated the loss of life that had made their paths cross, she was grateful that she had been able to talk him into working with her going forward.

The FBI trained agents better than any other law enforcement entity in the world, as far as Danielle was concerned. But they all had the same training. Too often, they all saw the same things, viewed it all through the same lens, and came to the same conclusions.

Morgan saw things through an entirely different lens. Apparently, a different lens than most of his colleagues as well. She'd done some checking, of course, before suggesting they work together again. He was known for taking the same set of facts presented to everyone else and coming to a unique and compelling finding that generally was right. He'd saved countless lives as a doctor. She had no doubt he'd be saving lives as a consultant for the FBI too. How many more people might the Georgetown Hospital Killer have taken out before the FBI had figured out what was going on if Morgan hadn't helped with the case?

Would those details he'd noticed on McNally's and Samson's bodies that the Medical Examiner had pretty much admitted he wouldn't have noticed end up being significant? Danielle didn't know the answer to that question, but she'd sure rather have chased down a lead that led nowhere than not have been given the lead at all.

"What will we be looking for at the scene?" Morgan asked. "The cops have been all over it already, haven't they?"

His tie went the way of his jacket and he unbuttoned the collar of his white dress shirt and rolled the sleeves up onto his corded forearms. There were a few beads of sweat at the edge of his tousled blond hair, but he still looked cooler than Danielle felt in her ubiquitous black suit.

Danielle nodded in answer to his question. "The police and the crime scene unit will have been over the area. I guess it's a little like you wanting to see those bodies. I need to be in the space. See it with my own eyes. Walk it myself."

"How did you end up connecting these two cases in the first place?" Morgan twisted in his seat to look at her.

Danielle tapped her finger against the steering wheel as she drove. "It wasn't really me. It was the detective who caught the cases for DC police. Two upper middle-class women of the same ethnicity and about the same age both killed by blunt force trauma within a couple of days of each other in the same city. Nothing stolen. No violent significant other. He asked me what I thought, and I thought it seemed worth looking into. It seems like I was right." That weird rash had been what tipped her over the edge.

"So a bit of a hunch?" he asked, one sandy blond eyebrow raised.

She smiled. "How about we call it an educated guess?"

He settled back in his seat, nodding. "I get that. I feel like that when I'm trying to make a diagnosis. Sure, I get gut feelings, but those gut feelings are based on things I've seen and learned."

"Exactly." She wasn't one to leap to conclusions, but she did often have those flashes of intuition that seemed to pan out. She might not know where the flashes came from when they happened, but she usually figured it out. Danielle pulled the sedan over to the curb. "We're here."

She stepped out of the air-conditioned vehicle into the swampy heat of a DC summer and immediately felt a drop of sweat trickle down her back. She wanted to keep her suit jacket on, though. No need to advertise to the neighborhood that she was carrying.

She turned to Morgan. "Normally, I would have come here first before going to the ME's office, but I guess that's what I get for teaming up with a doctor." She grinned at him. "Ready to come play in my sandbox?"

Morgan put on his own sunglasses. "Ready, boss."

CHAPTER FIVE

Morgan followed Danielle as she walked up to the uniformed police officer standing outside the crime scene tape that cordoned off the small parking lot and watched as she showed him her badge.

"Right. Detective Sheehan said to expect you." He took a step back to allow them both in, giving Morgan only a slightly curious glance.

The lot was shaped like an L with the short base of it tucked around the back of a building that held a cell phone repair shop. It would have been closed, of course, at the time of the attack. It was a small brick building with bars on the windows and a prominent sign showing that it was monitored 24/7 by an alarm company. Morgan wondered if the sign was a fake. As far as he could see, there were no security cameras. Everyone had those these days. Half his neighbors — now Ashley's neighbors, as he'd agreed to buy out his half of the house — out in Georgetown had some kind of doorbell camera or motion sensor camera trained on their porches and yards. He couldn't imagine a real security firm not placing cameras on a business they were supposed to protect.

It was obvious where the attack took place, tucked back out of sight of the street. The kind of beating that Angelica McNally took left a mess. Blood stained the gravel around what was nearly a white outline of a body. Clearly, McNally had already been down when most of the beating took place. Spatter from the attack went out in all directions, except in the direction that Morgan thought McNally's feet would have pointed.

It took him a moment and then he realized that the spatter in that direction would have been blocked by the assailant's body. That meant the blood spatter would have been on him.

"The guy would have been covered with blood," he said to Danielle. "Could he really just walk out of this parking lot and into the night with blood all over him? Carrying a bat? Wouldn't someone have noticed?"

Danielle walked over to the bloody outline of a body and looked around. She breathed in and let out a sigh. "It was two a.m. on a weeknight. There might not have been people around to avoid, but you

23

have a point. Or maybe he learned to bring a change of clothes with him. He would have known about the blood spatter after killing Kimberly Samson."

She crouched down and looked at the gravel at an angle, then stood and walked to the corner of the lot. "Or he might have had his own vehicle parked in the lot and had simply driven away when he was done. He walked this way after the attack."

"How do you know?"

Danielle pointed to a trail of blood drops across the gravel. "See how round those blood drops are? They dripped off something, most likely the murder weapon. He wasn't in any hurry, either. Compare them to the blood spray that was around the actual site of the murder. See how they're more elongated? That indicates a certain amount of velocity."

Morgan looked back and forth. Now that Danielle had pointed it out, the difference was obvious. He squinted at the line of blood drops. "Could those be tire tracks left by the killer?" Morgan pointed at a set of ruts nearby.

"Good eye on looking for a pattern, but I don't think so." Danielle walked over to stand next to him.

"Why not?"

Danielle crouched down again and pointed with a gloved hand at a few discolored spots on the gravel. "See those blood droplets? They were left after the tire marks were made. Otherwise, they would have been smeared. Those tire marks were here when the murder went down."

Morgan grimaced, chagrined. Of course. He should have realized that. Rookie mistake. Clearly.

"This is her car." Danielle indicated a Honda Civic parked in the corner, the driver's side door hanging open. "He didn't even bother to shut the door and he left his victim sprawled out here in the open. He's not trying to hide what he's doing in any way. It's almost as if he's trying to humiliate the victim further by leaving her out here to be found like that."

"What about Samson?" Morgan asked. "She was attacked in her home."

Danielle nodded. "And he left the front door of her house open. Anyone could have walked in and found her. He's testing the boundaries of what he can get away with and learning with each kill. The longer this goes on, the harder he will be to catch."

Morgan turned in a slow circle, trying to find something, anything that could help. Nothing seemed remarkable at the cell phone store or at McNally's car. His gaze snagged on the bar across the street. "Do we know where she was before she came to the parking lot?" he asked.

"We're still working on that," Danielle said. "We'll be able to figure out a lot more once we get all the cell phone data."

He pointed to the roofline of the bar. "There's a camera up there. Maybe it caught someone coming in or going out of this parking lot. The angle looks like it could work."

Danielle followed the direction that he pointed in and squinted, then looked up at him. "Good eye, Dr. Stark. Let's go find out what that camera caught."

CHAPTER SIX

Morgan looked up and down the street, trying to imagine getting into a vehicle and calmly driving away after having unleashed the holy hell that had taken Angelica McNally's life.

How could someone be that cold and also be possessed with the fury necessary to do what had been done to Angelica? He thought back to his psych rotation when he was a resident. Bipolar disorder didn't really fit. This switch between hypomania and a depressive episode didn't happen this quickly. Maybe Intermittent Explosive Disorder? The disorder's sudden explosive bouts of violence seemed to fit better with the two scenes, but people who suffered from the disorder were more impulsive. The scene at Samson's home and here in the parking lot seemed more controlled, planned.

Behind him, Danielle stopped to exchange a few words with the uniformed cop still standing guard at the entrance to the parking lot. "You can let Detective Sheehan know that we're done here. He can release the scene."

"Yes, ma'am." The officer stepped aside and pulled out his cell phone.

"Ready," Danielle said, stepping up next to him.

They walked across the street and let themselves into the bar. The cool darkness was an immediate relief from the scorching sun outside. Morgan took off his sunglasses and brushed a bead of sweat off his forehead.

"We're not open yet," a voice called from inside.

"You are for us," Danielle answered, holding up her badge. It glinted in the lowlight of the bar.

"Oh. Wow. Didn't realize, officer. Something I can help you with?" A white man came out from behind the bar. He was a big guy, well over six feet tall and probably weighing in at around 200 pounds, with one of those complicated spiky haircuts that seemed to require a lot of what Ashley always referred to as product. He wore an untucked button-down shirt that pulled at his shoulders and biceps.

A man like that could probably swing a bat pretty damn hard.

Danielle stuck out her hand. "Special Agent Hernandez. This is Dr.

Morgan Stark."

The man had a glass in one hand and a bar rag in the other. He held them up apologetically and didn't try to shake Danielle's hand. "Cory Smithson. Come on in. How can I help you?" He turned and walked back behind the bar.

Morgan followed him and sat down on one of the bar stools.

Danielle remained standing. "We're investigating an incident that happened last night in the parking lot across the street."

"Oh, yeah. I saw a bunch of cop cars and stuff there when I got in. I figured I should stay out of the way. MYOB, you know?" He pulled a rack of glasses out of the dishwasher and began drying them and putting them on shelves, stopping occasionally to rub at his forearm through his dress shirt.

"Good instinct," Danielle said, giving Smithson a brief smile. She pulled a photo of Angelica up on her phone and showed it to him. "Does this woman look familiar?"

Smithson's eyes widened and his face paled. "Totally. She was in here last night. Stayed until last call." He set the glass and rag down and rubbed his forearm.

"Did she talk to anyone? Leave with anyone?" Danielle leaned forward now.

Smithson grimaced. "I can't say for sure. I wasn't really paying a lot of attention to her. She wasn't a problem or anything. I don't think anyone was hassling her. I generally notice that kind of thing. We want the Tin Dog to be safe for everyone."

"Any chance we could take a look at the footage from the security camera you have out there?" Danielle pointed toward the door. "Just in case it caught something useful?"

Smithson blew out a breath. "I wish I could help you with that. That one's just for show."

Damn it. He thought he'd gotten Danielle a good lead there. At least they'd figured out where Angelica had spent part of her evening. "You said that one's for show," Morgan said, pointing to the camera he'd originally spotted. "Does that mean you have another one that isn't just for show?"

"You bet." Smithson said. "We've got one inside the bar."

"Could we see that footage?" Danielle asked.

"Of course. Follow me."

Smithson stepped out from behind the bar again, but this time led them down a hallway on the right past a store room and the restrooms to a small office, still rubbing at his forearm. Nervous habit? Or was there something wrong there? Morgan wasn't sure.

In the office, Smithson sat down behind the desk. Morgan and Danielle took the seats across from him. Smithson woke up the computer and started hitting buttons. "How far back do you want me to go?"

"When did she come in?" Danielle asked.

"Hmm. Not 100 percent certain." He rewound through a few hours and then stopped. "Here's where she comes up to the bar. I'm assuming it would be about when she came in. I don't remember her being at a table before that."

Smithson turned the computer monitor toward Danielle and Morgan. The angle of the camera was from up and to the left of where Angelica was sitting, but it was clearly her, although the scarf around her neck and the high neck of her shirt hid the rash and the bump on her neck. The timestamp read 11:15 p.m.

"Go ahead and speed it up," Danielle said, leaning forward to watch the video.

In fast motion, Smithson showed up in the video, took Angelica's order, and delivered her drink. As he reached across the bar to give her the drink, his sleeve rode up and Morgan thought he could see a red blotchy mark on the man's wrist. It was hard to tell for sure. He glanced over at Smithson, who rubbed at the same spot through his shirt, now, with a bit of a grimace.

A rash? Could it be the same kind of rash that Angelica and Kimberly had? What might that mean?

"She ordered a gin martini. Straight up. Nothing fancy, but not exactly weak," he said without prompting.

As they watched, Angelica pulled out her phone and set it on the bar next to her drink. Periodically, she'd tap on it.

"Any chance we can zoom in to see who she's texting with?" Morgan asked.

Smithson shook his head. "The quality of the video isn't that good. Plus it's dark."

On the video, Smithson served Angelica one more drink and then she put her phone back in her purse and stood up from the bar. There weren't many people left, but the few who were there did the same.

"That was last call," Smithson said.

The timestamp read 1:50 a.m.

No one had talked to Angelica for the two hours that she was there. Well, no one besides Smithson and whoever she was chatting with on the phone.

"Okay if I send that to our techs? They may be able to get more off it," Danielle said.

"Be my guest." Smithson moved the keyboard so Danielle could use it. She hit a few buttons and the computer made a whooshing noise as the email went off. Then turning to Morgan, she said, "We'll know once we get the phone records too. I've already got Divinia working on it."

"How did Ms. McNally seem to you?" Danielle turned back to Smithson. "Did she seem happy or nervous? Did you get the sense she was waiting for someone?"

Smithson shrugged. "She wasn't a regular, so I don't really have any kind of baseline. She seemed . . . normal."

Danielle sighed and stood. "Thank you for your time, Mr. Smithson." She pulled a card out of her pocket. "If you think of anything else, please give me a call."

When Smithson reached for the card, the shirt rode up on his arm again and Morgan could see the angry red rash there. No wonder he was rubbing at it. It probably itched like crazy. He wished he could see the rest of it, compare it more completely to the rash he'd seen on Angelica and Kimberly.

They followed Smithson back out into the bar, said their good-byes, and stepped back out onto the sidewalk.

Morgan pushed his hair back off his forehead. He probably needed to get it cut. Back in the old days, when they were starting out, Ashley used to cut it for him. It was one more thing that she'd quietly and efficiently done. He put his sunglasses on because of the glare and maybe a little to cover the mist that had welled up in his eyes.

He'd respected her wishes and signed the divorce papers. Intellectually, he knew it was over. He hoped it was just a matter of time before his heart figured it out too.

As they turned back toward the crime scene, a young woman with sleek black hair and tawny skin walked toward them. She had on tight jeans and a tank top with the bar's logo on the right breast. Morgan recognized her from the video footage they'd just watched. They'd seen her in the background, serving drinks and taking orders.

Danielle stepped in front of her and flashed her badge. The woman's eyes widened in alarm. Danielle was quick to reassure her. "You're not in any trouble. I just want to ask you some questions. Do you work here at the Tin Dog?"

The woman relaxed, settling her weight on one leg and putting her hands on her hips. "Yeah. What about it?"

Danielle ignored the attitude, although it made Morgan's eyebrows go up. "Did you work last night?"

"I did."

Danielle pulled up Angelica's picture on her phone again. "Do you remember this woman?"

The woman peered at the phone and then straightened back up. "Yeah. I remember her. Sat at the bar. Spent the whole night messaging with someone." She shook her head. "I thought it was weird. Why come out just to be on your phone? Booze is way cheaper at home."

She had a point. Why had Angelica bothered to come out if she was going to ignore her surroundings? Maybe she was hoping to meet someone and they never showed up?

Maybe they did show up, but not how Angelica expected. Morgan hoped Danielle's pull of Angelica's phone records would shed some light.

"Did you see anyone following her or anything? Did she get in any altercations with anyone?"

The cocktail waitress shook her head. "No. She was pretty polite. Not a bad tipper either."

"Anything odd that you may have noticed that didn't have anything to do with her?" Danielle asked.

Another head shake. "No. Not that I can think of. It was a normal night."

Normal. Smithson had used that same word to describe Angelica. Normal. So what had made her the murderer's intended victim? There had to be something, something that took her out of the ordinary for him, something that enraged him enough to attack with ferocity.

Danielle pulled out another card and handed it to the waitress. "If you think of anything, would you give me a call?"

The woman took the card and looked down at it. "What's this about anyway?"

Danielle pointed to the crime scene tape across the street. "It's about a murder."

The woman's face paled. "Murder? Like somebody got killed?"

"Yes. Exactly like somebody got killed." Danielle's voice was deadpan.

The waitress's eyes grew big again. "Who? That lady? The one who was on her phone all night?"

Danielle nodded. "So anything you saw or heard that seemed off or out of the ordinary would be helpful."

"Of course."

They started to walk away when Danielle turned and said, "Could we have your contact info? Just in case there's something we want to follow up on?"

"Sure. I'm Janelle Lewis." She pulled out a piece of paper from her bag and scrawled her number on it. "I'll think about it, but I doubt I'll come up with anything. Did you check the security cameras?" She pointed over Danielle and Morgan's shoulders at the camera over the bar door.

"The inside footage. Your boss said the outdoor camera was only for show," Morgan said.

The woman snorted. "Well, that's good to know. I guess I won't rely on that to keep me safe when I leave after last call." She tucked Danielle's card into her pocket. "I'll call if I think of anything, but I wouldn't count on it."

They continued to Danielle's car. "Do you really think the waitress will come up with anything useful?" Morgan asked, curious as to why Danielle bothered.

"It's a long shot, but you never know." She unlocked the car and they both got in. "Think of it this way. When you're trying to make a diagnosis and there's a test that may or may not give you the information you need, do you run it?"

"Of course. Sometimes a negative result gives you as much information as a positive one."

Danielle started the car. "Exactly."

Morgan buckled his seat belt and angled the air conditioning vents at his face. "I'm not sure if this means anything, but Smithson has a rash."

"What?" Danielle turned toward him. "How do you know?"

"It's on his forearm. He was rubbing at it and then I saw a little bit of it when he reached out to take your card. It's not on his chest like Angelica's and Kimberly's and I couldn't see enough of it to know whether it's the same kind of rash, but I thought I'd better mention it. It could be significant."

"Damn straight it could be," Danielle said and started the car.

CHAPTER SEVEN

Morgan got settled in the car, ready to go back to headquarters, but Danielle didn't put the car in gear. Instead, she pulled out her phone. "Hi, Henry. Did that video come through okay?"

She hit a button so Henry's voice came through the speaker in the car. "Yes, ma'am."

Morgan cocked his head as he listened. He knew this kind of underling. All polite and cooperative until you turned your back. He'd have to tell Danielle to watch hers. Or maybe he'd just do it for her.

"Great. Could you run a couple of names for me?" Danielle said to Henry.

"Sure."

"Cory Smithson. He's the owner of the Tin Dog. It's across the street from where Angelica McNally was killed. It's where she was before she was murdered."

"Got it."

"And Janelle Lewis. I've got a cell phone number for her, but not much else." Danielle used her phone to take a quick photo of the slip of paper Janelle had given her and then texted it to Henry.

"Danielle?" Divinia's voice came through the speaker. "Angelica's phone records came in."

"We'll be right there." Danielle hung up the phone and put the car in gear and they were on their way. "Did anything seem off to you about Smithson? Anything besides unexplained rashes on people's arms?"

Morgan thought back on their encounter. "He was a little bit blustery when we first walked in, but quieted down once he saw your badge."

"Good point. His first instinct was to try to bully us." Her dark eyes narrowed. "I've never liked a bully."

Leaving the car in the garage, they made their way into the FBI's headquarters. Up in the conference room, Divinia had a stack of paper in front of her that she was going through line by line, using a ruler to keep her place.

"Anything interesting?" Danielle asked as they walked in.

"Interesting? Yes. Helpful? Maybe not." Divinia turned the sheet of paper around to face Morgan and Danielle. She tapped the top number. "This is the last number Angelica texted with last night."

Morgan counted at least seven times the number appeared at the top of the list Divinia showed them.

"Who does it belong to?" Danielle asked.

Divinia pulled the papers back. "There's the bad news. It's a burner, which makes it nearly impossible to trace by the usual methods. We can still use cellular triangulation when it was in active use to determine where it was. That might end up being helpful."

Henry came back in the room, carrying some bags. "I've already started getting a warrant for the information." He unpacked sandwiches from the bags.

Morgan's stomach growled. He grabbed a sandwich marked turkey.

"Any idea what they texted about? It looked like she was on her phone for most of the time she was at the Tin Dog." Danielle grabbed a sandwich and unwrapped it as well.

Divinia pulled another stack of papers over. "You can see here that she made plans to meet this person over the weekend."

Morgan pulled the paper closer to him and read.

Angelica: So 8 p.m.?

Burner Phone: Sounds perfect. How will we find each other? That place gets crowded on the weekend.

Angelica: I'll wear a red top and black slacks.

Burner Phone: Sounds very sexy. You've peaked my interest.

He'd added a winky face emoji.

Angelica: Ha! We'll see. How will I know you?

Burner Phone: I'll be the devilishly handsome guy in a blue button-down and jeans.

Angelica: And, of course, we can text each other now.

Burner Phone: You got it.

Morgan looked up from the pages. "Peaked his interest?"

"He probably means piqued," Divinia said, around a bite of her own sandwich.

That made more sense. "This text string feels like it started up mid-conversation. Were they talking on the phone first? Or emailing?"

Divinia shook her head. "No. So far it's been all texting and that's the first time she's texted that number."

Danielle ran a long thin finger along the lines of text. "I see what you mean. So where else could this conversation have started if not by text or phone. They're exchanging details of what they'll be wearing so

33

I don't think they've met in person before."

"On an app?" Divinia suggested.

Danielle picked up another sheet of paper with details about Angelica's smartphone account. "Sheesh. She has like four pages of apps on this thing. I don't recognize at least half of them. It's going to take a while to sort through all that." She looked up at Divinia. "Want to follow that lead? Look for an app where this conversation might have started? Then see if you can get a subpoena to find out more about what Angelica was doing on it."

"Yes, ma'am." Divinia's face flushed a little.

Morgan looked back and forth between the two women, getting a better handle on the dynamics. Assigning Divinia to follow the lead on her own must have been a vote of confidence. That would explain Divinia's proud blush.

"I'd like to run a few other searches. Do you have this in a place where I can search what you've got?" Danielle asked.

"I'll send you the link right now." Divinia tapped at her keyboard.

Danielle opened her own laptop and started working in between bites of her sandwich. Morgan ate the rest of his own sandwich and grabbed a bag of chips, unsure of what he could add in the moment. His mind returned to the bodies of the two women. Something about those lipomas on their necks really bothered him. It felt like too big of a coincidence, especially with the added rash and possible jaundice. Nothing was coming to mind, though. He needed to do some research. He was about to suggest that he go back to his apartment and his own computer when Danielle sat back in her chair. "Angelica called the Tin Dog bar the day before she was killed."

Morgan wiped his hands on a napkin. "What does that mean?"

"No idea. Could be nothing. Could be something." She tapped an index finger against her lower lip. "She could have been checking their hours or something about their location or . . . Maybe she wanted to talk to someone there, someone she wanted to meet."

Morgan wasn't sure. There'd been nothing in Cory Smithson's behavior on the video that was suspicious. Lying about the camera and that rash, though? That was two strikes. "So what now?"

"Let's see if that waitress can tell us more about Smithson." Danielle pulled out her phone, dialed the number, and put the phone on speaker. "Hi, Janelle. This is Special Agent Hernandez with the FBI. We met this morning outside the Tin Dog. Can you talk?" Danielle asked.

"Um. Call back in five minutes. It's almost time for my break."

Danielle hung up and set the timer on her phone, then got up and stretched, lifting her arms over her head and swaying like a willow in the wind.

Henry looked up from his computer. "You're going to want to hear this, boss. Mr. Smithson had a statutory rape charge brought against him two years ago."

Danielle stopped swaying. She let her arms drop and looked at Henry. "What happened?"

Henry handed some papers fresh off the printer in the corner to her.

Danielle pinched her lower lip as she read. "Looks like some high school kids came into the bar using fake IDs. Smithson offered to look the other way in exchange for certain favors, shall we say."

Morgan's stomach rolled. Three strikes. "That's disgusting." He didn't understand men who behaved that way. They made him sick.

"And way too common," Danielle observed.

"What ended up happening?" Divinia had set her pen and ruler down to listen.

"The women dropped the charges. They didn't want to deal with potentially having used fake IDs on their own records or pay the fines or do the community service work," Danielle said. She dropped the stack of papers down. "They're young. They didn't want this following them around for the rest of their lives."

Maybe Smithson liked them young. "Angelica looked young for her age. Do you think Smithson might have hit on her? Gotten angry when she said no?" Morgan asked. But then how was he connected with Kimberly? It wasn't adding up, but there was still something wrong there.

"Or made too aggressive a move and then didn't want her reporting him? Having a second sexual offense brought against you isn't exactly going to be good for business or life style." Danielle was tapping her index finger against her lips again.

"So what do we do now?" Morgan asked.

"Looks like we're going back to the Tin Dog. We'll talk to Janelle on our way."

Once they were back in the car and out of the garage, Danielle put the phone on speaker and hit redial to call Janelle. It was late afternoon and it had clouded over. A few spits of rain hit the windshield.

"What can you tell us about your boss?" Danielle asked after the waitress answered.

"Cory?" There was a whooshing sound that Morgan was pretty sure was the sound of Janelle inhaling cigarette smoke, then another whoosh

35

as she blew it out. "As guys who own bars go, he's not bad. Why?"

"It looks like our murder victim called the bar the afternoon before she was killed," Danielle said.

"Really?" Janelle sounded surprised.

"Really. You're sure you haven't seen her in there before?"

"No. We get a lot of people who come through here. I'm not going to remember every face." She took another drag on her cigarette.

Fair point, but if she was a regular, wouldn't she have become noticeable?

"Did you see her talking to your boss at all?" Danielle asked.

"He mixed drinks for her, but no chitchat beyond taking her order. At least, not that I saw." There was a pause. "Look. Smithson's okay. Like I said, as far as bar owners go, he's all right, but, well, let's just say he's not running in a strong field."

Danielle glanced over at Morgan with her eyebrows raised. "What does that mean?"

"That means a lot of people who run places like this aren't the greatest. Smithson can definitely be a little bit of a creep. I've caught him trying to look down the front of my tank top a few times. The tank top he insists all the female employees wear, by the way. Stuff like that. He's never tried to cop a feel or anything like that, though." Janelle seemed to think that amounted to high praise. She took another drag on her cigarette.

"Any chance he could have followed her out?" Danielle asked.

"I sure didn't see him do that." There was another pause accompanied by a loud sigh. "Look. I know he told you that camera outside was for show, but that's bull. I don't know why he told you that. I've looked at video from it before so it definitely worked at some point."

"That's really good to know, Janelle. Thank you."

"Whatever. I gotta go. Could you do me a favor? Don't mention that I've talked to you, okay? This is a decent gig. I don't want to screw that up."

"Sure. No problem."

Danielle hit the disconnect button. "What do you think?"

"I think there's a lot more wrong with Smithson than a rash." A whole lot more.

Danielle pulled the SUV into the alley behind the bar. An F250 was parked in one of the two spaces. She parked directly behind it, effectively blocking it in. As they got out of the car, Smithson walked out, carrying a bag of garbage, headed to the Dumpster.

Danielle stepped out of the car. "Cory Smithson, we have a few more questions for you."

He started and then turned, frowning. "About what?"

"Let's start with why Angelica McNally called your bar the afternoon of the same evening she was murdered." Danielle's voice was conversational, almost as if she was asking about the weather. It didn't fool Morgan one bit. She let Smithson get to the Dumpster and throw his trash in, then she took a few steps to the left. With a head nod to Morgan, she indicated that he should take up a post to the right. He wasn't sure why, but he cooperated.

Smithson's eyebrows drew down. "She did?"

"She did. She spoke to someone here for around three-and-a-half minutes. Too long for a voicemail."

Smithson shook his head. "I can't tell you. Lots of people call asking about hours and directions and parking. Stuff like that. It was probably that."

He made a move to go around Danielle, but she sidestepped to block his passage. "Okay. How about we talk about that camera out front?"

Smithson's Adam's apple bobbed up and down. "What about it?" He took some steps to the right. This time, Morgan stepped forward into his path. His mouth went dry. Doctors argued. Sure, their arguments even got heated on occasion. They didn't get physical, though. If Smithson took a swing at him, he wasn't sure what he would do or, more importantly, what he should do.

"Why did you disable it?" Danielle asked.

"What?" Smithson looked down at his feet. "No. It's not what you think."

"How about you come with us and tell us exactly what it is then?" Danielle stepped aside opening a path for Smithson to walk to the car. Instead, he tried to dodge around Danielle.

He was going to run. Danielle stepped to his left so Morgan went right, his heart rate zooming up despite barely moving.

Morgan could see it now. Everything that Danielle had done since they arrived had been making sure they were ready for this moment. The way she'd positioned the car by the truck and the Dumpster. Where she'd stood and where she'd indicated Morgan should stand. She'd known exactly what Smithson was likely to do and had all the contingencies accounted for.

Smithson made one more attempt at trying to get around Danielle. This time, she grabbed his arm and twisted it up behind his back.

Smithson wilted. "Fine. I'll come with you."

"Good choice, Mr. Smithson." Danielle pulled out her phone and called to let Henry and Divinia know they were bringing someone in for questioning.

Morgan felt the starch go out of his spine. Smithson was a big guy, broad-shouldered and muscular. If he'd decided to put up a fight, Morgan wasn't sure what he could have done to be helpful.

He'd seen Danielle bring someone down with a twist of her wrist, but the size and weight differential here was considerable. If she hadn't been able to subdue him, what could Morgan have done besides look mean?

Nothing. He hadn't been in a physical fight since second grade when Max Wallace accused him of cheating at four square. There were certain skill sets that would be good to have for this consulting gig that he simply didn't have yet.

He was going to have to look into doing something about that.

Right after they caught whoever murdered Kimberly Samson and Angelica McNally.

CHAPTER EIGHT

Interrogation techniques were one more thing Morgan needed to learn more about. He stood with Danielle outside the interview room where Smithson was currently sitting, handcuffed to a metal bar imbedded in the table. "Am I going in with you?" he asked. He wanted to, but he wasn't sure what he could offer.

Danielle looked him up and down. "Think you can keep your cool?"

Morgan looked down at his feet. He hadn't exactly acquitted himself well in previous interrogations, but he wasn't as personally involved in this case as he had been in that one. When he'd thought he was talking to the person who had murdered someone he had cared about, he'd let his emotions get the best of him. He was outraged for Kimberly and Angelica, but he felt he could take that step back that would let him hold his temper. "I can."

Danielle bit her lower lip. "Want to be the good cop?"

Morgan's head shot up. "Seriously? What would I do?"

"You know. Just establish some rapport with him. Connect with him if you can. Get him to trust you." She tugged her jacket down and nodded. "While I tear him a new one."

"To what end?" Morgan asked, wanting to understand what he should do.

"He'll look to you for help. He'll still perceive us as a team, but he'll think you're the reasonable one who could intercede for him." She opened the door to the room, letting it bang against the wall and making Smithson jump.

Morgan followed Danielle into the interrogation room.

"So Mr. Smithson," Danielle sat down and tapped the file folders in front of her into a neat stack. "Did you know that lying to the FBI is a federal offense punishable by up to five years in prison?"

Smithson pushed back hard in his chair. "Wait! What?"

"Five years in a federal prison. Not to mention the fines." Danielle crossed her arms over her chest. "Doesn't even have to be about covering up a crime. Lying to us will send you to prison."

Danielle gave Morgan a little kick under the table and glanced at him out of the side of her eyes. He sat up and broke in. "Look, man. Why don't you help us out? I'm sure if you tell us the truth now, Special Agent Hernandez here will reconsider charging you." He turned to Danielle. "Right, Agent Hernandez?"

She made a hmmphing noise.

Smithson rubbed hard at his forearm. "Please. I-I-I was scared."

"Scared that we'd find out about how you like trying to coerce young women into performing sex acts on you?" Danielle asked, her eyes wide and innocent.

Smithson's chin began to tremble. "Those charges were dropped!"

"Doesn't mean they didn't happen, though, did it?" Danielle said, leaning in now. "So now we've established that you're a perv, did you follow Angelica out of the bar at closing? Did you corner her by her car and when she turned you down, did you beat her to death? Then did you go back to the bar and erase the video of you following her?"

"No no no no no." Smithson almost wailed, scratching hard at his forearm. "No. I didn't. I wouldn't't."

Danielle shook her head. "Yeah. I'm pretty sure you would."

"Can I see your arm?" Morgan asked.

"My what?" Smithson looked confused at the sudden change in topic.

Danielle sat back, watching to see where he was going.

"Your arm. Where you're scratching." Morgan pointed at Smithson's forearm.

Smithson turned up his shirtsleeve. Morgan reached across and pulled Smithson's arm toward him, turning it this way and that. Damn it. It wasn't even close to the rash he'd seen on Angelica and Kimberly. It wasn't the same thing at all. It did look pretty angry, though. "How long have you had the rash?"

Smithson shrugged. "A few weeks now."

"Does it itch?"

"Like crazy, man. I keep putting stuff on it." Smithson went to scratch at it again, but Morgan stopped his hand.

"What kind of stuff?"

"Hydrocortisone cream. Stuff for athlete's foot."

"Over-the-counter medications?" Morgan shook his head. "That's eczema. Most likely discoid eczema based on those circular marks. Those creams you've been using aren't going to help. You need an antibiotic. Something like mupirocin." He let go of Smithson's arm.

"Where can I get that?" Smithson asked.

"You'll need to ask your doctor. It's prescription, but it'll clear that up in about a week. You should do it before it spreads, though."

Smithson rolled his sleeve back down. "Thanks, man."

"Well, now that we've had this nice episode of Name that Rash, could we get back to how Mr. Smithson murdered Angelica McNally?" Danielle asked.

Smithson went back into panic mode. "No! I swear. I didn't hurt that woman. I served her a couple of drinks. That's it." He turned back to Morgan, eyes wide and pleading.

Danielle continued as if he hadn't even spoken. "Pretty convenient that you disabled that camera out front so we couldn't see you follow her. I understand that this business about it being a fake is a big fat lie."

Smithson looked over at Morgan who held up his hands. "Sorry, man. I can't help you with this one. You're going to have to explain why you lied. It's the only way out of this."

Smithson turned back to Danielle. "I was rebooting the system. I had to turn the cameras off. It takes a while and I wanted it to be done before I went home, so I turned the outside one off right before closing. I swear. I wasn't trying to cover anything up. I swear I didn't do anything to that woman. I wouldn't."

Danielle made a noise in the back of her throat like she was about as likely to buy that as she was to buy the Brooklyn Bridge. Before she could go any further, though, there was a discreet knock at the door and Henry stuck his head in.

"Something you should see, boss."

Danielle stood and indicated that Morgan should follow her out of the room. After the door shut, she said, "Nice touch with the rash. Diagnosing skin problems during interrogation might be taking good cop a little far, but it definitely threw him off his game."

"I wanted to see if his rash was anything like what we saw on Angelica and Kimberly. It's not."

"But then you gave him treatment options!" Danielle laughed. "It was quite the performance."

"The guy was clearly suffering." The fact that he could be a murderer didn't enter into Morgan's calculations on whether or not he should provide medical help. Morgan leaned back against the wall.

Danielle turned to Henry. "What've you got, Henry?"

"I was going through the video footage you sent from inside the bar. I don't think Smithson's our man." He walked back to the conference room.

Once in the room, Henry hit a few buttons to wake up his laptop. "Watch this." He hit the play button and they watched Angelica

41

McNally finish her martini and pay her bill.

"I didn't see Smithson on the tape after that point," Danielle said. "Without being able to see her walk out the door without anyone following her, it's hard to know if he did or didn't."

"That's what I thought when I watched it the first time." Henry pointed at an area of the bar. "Watch here."

The image brightened as lights came on in the bar, probably to make cleaning up and shutting down easier. It also created a reflection in the polished wood of the countertop. "Damn it," Danielle said. "There he is."

Smithson's reflection was surprisingly clear in the video.

"He moves in and out of frame a few times, but never for more than a few minutes at a time. It's after three by the time he shuts everything down and leaves. There's no way he was gone long enough to follow McNally to the parking lot and to . . . do what was done to her," Henry said. The young agent was clearly as upset by what had happened to Angelica McNally as Morgan was.

Danielle sighed. "Back to the drawing board. Literally," she said, looking up at the whiteboards with Angelica McNally and Kimberly Samson's photos looking down at them. "Henry, go release Mr. Smithson. Arrange a ride back to the bar for him."

Outside, the rain had started in earnest, fat drops streaking down the windows of the conference room. A crack of thunder boomed in the distance.

Danielle turned to Morgan. "There's not much else we can do today. Might as well head home and get a decent night's sleep so we can start fresh tomorrow." She slumped a little against the table.

"How?" Morgan asked. What other leads did they have to follow?

"We need to learn more about the victims themselves. We need to find that connection, the nexus that brought them both into this killer's sights." She knocked twice on the table as if she'd made a decision and then pulled her ponytail tighter. "How do you feel about road trips?"

CHAPTER NINE

The man punched the number the woman had given him into his phone and waited. One ring. Two. She was expecting his call. Apparently, she didn't want to seem too eager. The games these women played. It was like they'd all read the same book and followed its advice to the letter. He didn't mind. It made them predictable. The phone rang a third time and this time she answered. "Hello?"

"Hi! Is this Sandra?" He looked at her photo as he spoke to her. Did she really think that high-necked shirt was going to fool anyone? Did she think it make her look demure?

"Sure is. Is this Luke?"

The man smiled. He'd heard that people could tell if you were smiling on the other end of the phone, whether or not they could see you. "Thanks for taking my call."

She giggled. "It seemed like it was time to take it to the next level."

He kept the smile plastered on his face, but his shoulders tensed. Of course she thought it was time to go to the next level, even though it had only been a couple of days. She was a slut after all. Weren't they always ready to go to the next level? He was surprised it had taken her this long. "I'm flattered."

"You should be." She giggled again. "I'm picky."

Not that picky. She was like all of them. Ready to go with whomever, whenever. "Well, I'm picky too." He picked up a pair of scissors that were lying on his desk and jabbed them as hard as he could into the wooden surface. It made a satisfying thunk.

"What was that? Are you okay?"

"Oh, nothing. Just some construction work going on outside." He jammed the scissors into the desk again.

"Got it. So, did you want to meet up? Maybe have coffee?"

So now she was going to play coy? Coffee? Please. "Sure. Coffee would be great, but how about we go for a walk first. Have you ever been to the arboretum?"

"Never been there, but I'm always willing to try something new." She giggled again, and he stabbed the desk again, imaging now that it was her face.

"Great. How about two o'clock? I'll text you the address."

"I'm looking forward to it."

"Me too," he lied. Well, maybe it wasn't a lie. He was looking forward to it. He'd been surprised at how satisfying it had been to make those two other women pay for their sins.

It would be a pleasure to make this one pay too. They hung up and he turned to the corner where his baseball bat leaned against the wall.

CHAPTER TEN

Morgan was waiting outside when Danielle pulled up. She'd texted him that morning that she'd pick him up at eleven, that she had some digging to do and some appointments to set up for them.

He'd spent a frustrating morning waiting for the time that she'd arrive. He'd gone for a run, showered, ate, done some laundry, and paid some bills. Was this what it was going to be like if he wasn't going into the hospital every day? He wasn't sure he'd be able to take it. He needed some focus, a goal. He'd lived his whole life always working toward something.

How would he fill the hours in the day?

He spent what felt like a useless hour researching, trying to find something that would connect all the symptoms he'd seen in Kimberly and Angelica. Maybe he'd know more once they got the results of their autopsies. He certainly hoped so. Right now there were too many possibilities and none pointed to anything that could have gotten them murdered.

Morgan got in the car as soon as Danielle pulled to a stop at the curb. "So, where are we headed?"

"Philadelphia."

His eyebrows went up. That was close to three hours if the traffic cooperated, and the traffic never really cooperated. At least the rain had stopped. The air still felt sticky, but the sun was doing its best to burn off some of the cloud cover.

"I thought about flying, but by the time we got to the airport, went through everything there, got to Philly, and then rented a car, well, it would be about the same amount of time." She shrugged. "Besides, this way we can come and go when we please."

And have more control. Morgan was beginning to understand how Danielle's mind worked. He got it. The best way to figure out the right answer was to control as many of the variables as you could. He'd been accused of being a control freak more than once in his life.

"So what's in Philadelphia besides good cheese steak and the Liberty Bell?" Morgan asked.

"Angelica McNally's family." Her index finger tapped on the

45

steering wheel, a sure sign that she was still thinking through something.

"What are we hoping to learn from meeting Angelica's family?" Morgan asked. If they lived as far away as Philadelphia, how much would they know about Angelica's day-to-day life? That was what they needed to know about.

Danielle thought for a moment before answering. "What's the first thing you do when a new patient comes to you?"

"Besides assess vitals and do some basic blood work? Generally, we get a family history." Morgan looked out the window at the landscape whizzing by, green and lush.

"Why?" Danielle pushed.

Morgan turned to look at her. "Because a lot of the time, whatever is going wrong has its roots in the person's genetic makeup or possibly even environmental factors from where they grew up."

"Mmhmm." Danielle smiled. "Think of this as taking a family history. A lot of times the reason someone decided to make this person a victim of a crime has its roots in who they were, what they did, where they worked, or where they're from. They got where they were for a reason, through a series of steps. By digging into Angelica's and Kimberly's lives, we might find the connection between them and why whoever this madman is decided to attack them. Speaking of which, I'm going to call Kimberly Samson's parents as we drive. Detective Sheehan already talked to them and didn't get much, but you never know what you might shake loose if you keep pressing."

"So they're local?" Morgan asked. "What do they do?"

Danielle squinted as she tried to remember. "Dad is a professor of something. Political science, I think? Mom is in administration of a non-profit that brings arts programs to inner city schools."

Morgan sank back in his seat while Danielle hit a few buttons. The sound of a ringing telephone came through the speakers in the car radio.

"Hello, Ms. Samson, this is Special Agent Danielle Hernandez of the FBI."

There was a long pause and then a cool voice said, "What the hell does the FBI want with me?"

Instant hostility. Not exactly what Morgan expected.

"I'd like to talk to you about your daughter Kimberly," Danielle said.

There was a sharp intake of breath. "My daughter is dead, Agent. There's nothing else to discuss."

46

"Wait. Ms. Samson, I want to find out who killed your daughter," Danielle said.

Samson sniffed. "I've already talked to the police. They've given me the impression that there's nothing they can do. Typical law enforcement."

So, she had a thing against law enforcement? He typed the names into a search function on his phone. Professional profiles popped up for both parents. They were a little older than he expected, but that explained it. They were only a few years too young to have been flower children back in the sixties. They'd grown up on not trusting law enforcement or anyone over thirty. Apparently, the not trusting law enforcement thing had stuck.

"I'm sorry they gave you that impression. I think we have some new leads. We think whoever killed your daughter might have also killed another woman," Danielle explained.

There was a sharp intake of breath. "What? Who? When?"

That seemed to get through to her.

"I'm afraid I can't discuss the details, but I was hoping you would talk to us to see if we can find a connection between your daughter and the other victim. It might help us find whoever did this."

"What do you mean by we?" The suspicion had returned to Ms. Samson's voice.

"I'm in the car with Dr. Morgan Stark. He's consulting on the case with us." Danielle gestured to Morgan.

"Hello, Ms. Samson. Dr. Stark here. Thank you for taking the time to talk to us," Morgan leaned forward to make sure she could hear him.

Samson continued as if Morgan hadn't spoken. "Why a doctor? Kimberly was a healthy young woman."

And she was back to arguing with everything.

Morgan broke in. "I'm sure she was, Ms. Samson. I'm here to consult in case something comes up." He glanced over at Danielle. She gave him a nod of approval.

Ms. Samson sniffed again. "Sounds a little fishy to me, but go ahead. Ask your questions."

Morgan supposed that was progress.

"Was there any change in your daughter's demeanor lately? Did she seem upset about anything? Nervous?" Danielle asked.

"Upset? No. Not really." She dragged the last word out a little as if she was reconsidering it as she said it.

Morgan noticed the selective response. Danielle must have too. They exchanged glances. "Maybe something besides upset?"

A noisy sigh came over the line. "She'd been . . . cagey lately."

"How do you mean cagey?" he asked.

"Like everyone means it, Dr. Stark." Samson's tone went sharp. She must be a joy to work for. "She'd been less forthcoming than usual about her schedule, her whereabouts. To be honest, I thought she'd started seeing someone."

That was interesting. Kimberly might have recently started dating someone. Angelica had been at a bar and had been texting someone about meeting up. Was there some kind of connection there?

Danielle clearly caught the connection too, as her eyebrows went up. "What made you think that?"

"She seemed to have some kind of standing date on Thursday nights. It took me a while to notice, but she was never available on Thursday nights between 7 and 9."

"And that was new?" Danielle asked.

"Yes. It was also new that she wouldn't tell me where she was," Samson sighed. "I didn't push it. She was a grown woman and entitled to some privacy, but she'd always been forthcoming before. We'd been so close." There was a small catch in Samson's voice, the first sign of her true emotions about her daughter's death. Maybe all the bluster had been to cover up that vulnerability.

"Did it concern you that she wasn't telling you about it?" Danielle asked.

"No. Actually, I was happy for her. She hadn't been dating much recently. She had a bad break-up a while back. A boyfriend who cheated on her. She'd seemed reluctant to get out there again. I'd actually tried to fix her up with a friend's son, and she got quite angry with me, told me that I didn't understand."

"Didn't understand what?" Morgan asked. What precisely did that mean and could it have a bearing on the case? What kind of secrets was Kimberly Samson keeping from her mother?

"She wouldn't say, but I backed off. When I realized that she had started having these regular Thursday night engagements, well, I crossed my fingers, hoped for the best, and didn't ask too many questions." Again, there was that catch in her voice. "I just wanted her to be happy."

Danielle's index finger was tapping out its secret rhythm on the steering wheel again. "Thank you for your time, Ms. Samson. I appreciate it."

"Agent Hernandez?" Helena Samson's voice had gotten smaller and significantly softer.

48

"Yes?"

"Do you think that whatever she was doing on Thursday nights could have contributed to her death? Should I have pushed her to tell me more?" The slight catch in her voice had grown to a quaver.

Ah, there was the other thing the bluster had probably been meant to cover. Guilt.

Danielle said, "If her Thursday night appointment has any relevance to her death, I doubt you having pushed Kimberly to tell you about it would have made any difference. There was no way for you to know what would happen."

"Thank you, Agent. I just . . . I couldn't bear the thought that I maybe could have stopped this from happening."

Morgan's heart broke a little, hearing this proud haughty woman brought low by her grief. He had no children himself. Ashley had wanted to have kids, but he hadn't been ready. It was selfish, really. He didn't want to change how he lived and he knew a baby would be a huge change. He hoped Ashley still had time. He hoped it wasn't one more thing he'd taken from her and given nothing in return.

"I appreciate your help, Ms. Samson. We'll be back in touch if we find anything out." Danielle was wrapping up the phone call.

"Thank you."

They hung up. "Do you think there's some kind of connection there? Between Kimberly possibly having a new boyfriend in her life and Angelica making arrangements to meet someone?" Morgan asked "Could they have been getting involved with the same person?" And could that person be their culprit?

"Possibly." Danielle hit buttons again and soon Divinia's voice was coming over the car's speakers.

"Hi, Danielle. What can I do for you?"

"Divinia, could you check to see if there are any phone number that both Kimberly and Angelica called?"

"Sure thing. I'll do some searches and get back to you."

The McNally home was a well-renovated Philadelphia row house i Society Hill, made of red brick with stone detailing over arche windows. The McNallys had an end-unit that still had the origin stained glass detailing over the front door. It might sound modest, b Morgan knew enough about real estate to recognize a highly desirabl neighborhood that would come with a steep price tag.

The second they got out of the car, the humidity instantly mac Morgan's shirt stick to his back. If the humidity bothered Danielle, sh didn't show it. She unlocked the glove box to retrieve her servi weapon, and then retrieved her suit jacket from the back seat where it had been carefully folded. She marched up to the door and knocked. "They're expecting us."

Morgan walked up the steps to stand slightly behind and to Danielle's left. A short blonde woman with red-rimmed blue eyes opened the door. She had on what Ashley always called athleisure wear: capri-length leggings and a tank top of moisture-wicking material, stretchy and comfortable, but too nice to actually work out in.

Danielle held up her badge. "Mrs. McNally? I'm Special Agent Hernandez and this is my associate, Dr. Stark."

She blinked at them for a moment or two as if she was having some trouble processing what was being said to her. Finally, she said, "Oh, of course. Yes. Come in. Please."

She opened the door wider and they stepped inside into the cool air-conditioned air.

"Let me just get Ed." She turned away from them and walked up the stairs. "Ed," she called. "The FBI lady is here."

She motioned for them to follow her into the living room, furnished with a contemporary-looking sectional sofa and a big screen television. "He'll be down in a minute. Can I get you anything? Coffee? Water?"

"Water would be great," Morgan said.

"Yes. That would be lovely," Danielle said.

A row of photos stood on a credenza under the window. Morgan recognized Angelica from the photo Danielle had tacked to the top of their whiteboard. She looked like her mother. Pretty. A little plump. Cupid's bow mouth and blue eyes. There was a photo of her in a cap and gown, another of her waterskiing behind a motor boat. There were photos of another young woman, most likely a sister, in a wedding gown.

An older man walked into the room and looked back and forth between Danielle on the couch and Morgan over by the photos. He had dark hair with a touch of gray at his temples and wore khaki shorts with a light blue Polo shirt. He peered at them through rimless glasses. "Hello. Can I help you?"

Mrs. McNally came in then. "Ed, that's the FBI lady. The one who called earlier. I'm sorry. What was your name again?" She handed Danielle one of the glasses of water she was carrying.

"Hernandez. Special Agent Danielle Hernandez." Danielle took the glass. She took out a card and handed it to Mrs. McNally.

Morgan stepped forward and stuck out his hand. "Morgan Stark."

Ed McNally shook it and then slumped down in the wingback chair that faced the sectional sofa at an angle. "So, what can we do for you?"

Mrs. McNally perched next to him on the arm of the chair. "Yes. Anything we can do." She pulled a tissue out of her pocket and dabbed at her eyes. Her husband put a steadying hand on her thigh.

"What can you tell me about Angelica in the last few months?" Danielle asked. "Did anything seem off to you? Was she more anxious than normal?"

The couple exchanged glances. "I'm not sure we would have known if she was," Ed said. "Angelica hadn't been around much recently."

Danielle cast a sidelong glance at Morgan and then asked, "Any reason for that?"

If Angelica had been putting her energy into dating in DC, she might not have wanted to spend a lot of time in Philadelphia with her parents.

"Oh, you know kids these days," Mrs. McNally said. "They have to sow those wild oats. Get all that out of their system so they can settle down." She glanced over at the photos of her daughters and a little sob escaped her.

Morgan looked down at his shoes. Mr. McNally would never walk Angelica down the aisle as he had with her older sister. Mrs. McNally would never be the one to put those final touches on her daughter's veil and dress. They'd been robbed of that by someone.

"I'll — I'll be right back." Mrs. McNally left the room.

Mr. McNally dropped his chin to his chest. "Sorry."

"Don't be," Morgan said. "It's only human." Everyone grieved in their own way. He'd seen that with his own parents after his sister's disappearance and all too many times in the hospital. Needing a few minutes to calm yourself enough to speak to law enforcement about your daughter's murder seemed completely understandable.

"I suppose so." McNally sighed. "I'm not sure what else to tell you."

Danielle hesitated. Morgan thought about what Kimberly's mother had said about a standing date on Thursday nights. Could that have been something that connected the two women? Maybe some kind of singles gathering?

"Did Angelica have any kind of standing appointment or date on Thursdays?" Morgan asked. Maybe they'd find some kind of connection there. It was the only thing that really stood out about what Kimberly Samson's mother had told them.

McNally had taken his glasses off and was polishing their lenses on the hem of his Polo shirt. "Oh. You mean her art class."

"Art class?" That hadn't been what Morgan had expected. Maybe there was no connection, but if both women were going out on Thursday nights for something, maybe their paths had crossed somehow.

McNally pinched the bridge of his nose. "Art class or maybe it was something else. I can't remember if she ever really explained what it was. Last time she was home, I noticed one of those parking passes stuck in the window of her car for the community center near her apartment. I asked her about it, and she made some kind of joke. Said she was taking an underwater basket weaving class."

Had Angelica used a joke to deflect questions about what she was really doing with her Thursday nights? Was she being cagey like Kimberly had been with her mother? Maybe they'd found another lead to follow. What might both women have been hiding from their families? New loves in their lives? Something less savory? Danielle had been right about digging into the victim's lives to find that nexus.

They stood. Danielle, as always, offered McNally her card even though she'd already given one to his wife. "Please call if you think of anything else." She paused. "And please apologize to your wife. We didn't mean to upset her."

McNally waved the apology off. "You're doing your job. We appreciate that." Then a change came over the man's face. Gone was the affable, slightly out of focus look. The only way Morgan could think to describe it was that McNally's face became murderous. "I hope you catch the bastard who did this to my baby. Then I hope you'll leave me in a room with him alone for ten minutes."

CHAPTER ELEVEN

Morgan's stomach growled loud enough that Danielle gave him a sidelong look. He put his hand against the offending organ and winced.

"Hungry?" she asked.

"Starving." He blushed a little. It seemed like Danielle could run all day on a few cups of coffee and the occasional energy bar. He needed more sustenance.

She pulled off the Interstate and found a chain restaurant where they could at least sit down to order. Once they were settled in a booth, the waitress came by and Morgan listened to Danielle order a cheeseburger with French fries. He ordered a salad with grilled chicken. She whipped out her phone and her notebook.

"We'll hit the community center tomorrow morning. I had Henry call and set up an appointment with the director for us," Danielle told him.

It was past ten o'clock by the time Danielle dropped Morgan back at his apartment.

"Aren't you exhausted?" She looked more tired than he remembered seeing her before. There were dark circles under her eyes and a droop to her shoulders. He was tired too, but that was part of the gig when you were a doctor. He'd been pushing through fatigue for years.

She shrugged. "You get used to it. When I'm working on a case like this, I can't seem to ever turn it off so I might as well make some progress."

Morgan was well aware of what that was like. "See you in the morning."

He unlocked the door to his apartment building and waved to Danielle, who gave a quick double toot of her horn and then left.

He stopped at the mailboxes. Pretty much nothing but junk mail and ad circulars. Not even a bill. Those all came electronically these days. Unsure of why that depressed him, Morgan took the stairs up to his floor and let himself into the apartment. The air had that stale quality empty places get sometimes. Sighing, he punched the air conditioning

53

down a bit to get some air moving.

He pulled his keys and wallet out of his pockets to put them on his dresser and noticed that he'd missed a call on his phone. He'd turned it to silent when they'd gone in to speak to the McNallys, and he'd forgotten to turn it back on.

He pressed the button to see who had called.

Ashley. Of course she'd called.

He listened to the voicemail she'd left. "Hi, Morgan. I wanted to see how you were doing. I know the hearing didn't go the way you wanted it to. If you need to talk, I'm here." The sweet lilt of her voice made him smile.

It was hard to believe the hearing on whether or not he would be able to continue practicing medicine at Georgetown or anywhere else, for that matter, had been only the day before. It seemed like a lifetime ago. He'd barely thought about it since he walked out of the hospital with Danielle. He'd been too caught up in the case.

He wasn't sure what that meant. Maybe it was the novelty of working with law enforcement. Maybe it was something more. Maybe it was time to think about making a real change in his life.

In the past, with a big decision like that, he'd have talked it over with Ashley. She was a great listener, but more than that, she asked great questions. She had this way of asking him things that made him look at the issue differently and helped him get truly to the heart of whatever it was.

He missed that.

He glanced up at the clock. Nearly eleven o'clock on a weeknight. She was almost certainly in bed. Just in case, he shot off a quick text. He watched for a moment, but no little gray dots appeared. She was probably already asleep.

She'd often gone to bed before him. Sometimes before he even got home. He'd shower to get all the hospital smells and germs off of himself and then slip into bed, spooning up behind her.

Some nights, he'd kiss that little place where her neck met her shoulder, the spot that made her wriggle against him. Then she'd turn to him, sweet and warm with sleep, smelling like the lavender lotion she used on her hands and feet and tasting like heaven.

He shook his head to clear it. There was no use letting his mind wander down those particular pathways. He was lucky Ashley still cared about him at all. He doubted that would extend to inviting him back into her bed.

A guy could hope and dream, though.

He grabbed a beer from the refrigerator, popped off the cap, and took a long pull, letting the cold liquid soothe his throat. He held the bottle against his forehead, appreciating the cool glass.

He was being ridiculous. There were other people he could talk to. Sure, his marriage hadn't worked out, but that didn't mean he was some kind of pariah. He had friends, didn't he? Maybe he'd call someone right now rather than sitting here feeling sorry for himself.

The last time he'd felt like he was losing his mind, he'd called his old mentor Monte Flint. On impulse, he pulled out his phone and pressed the button to call him.

After four rings, he heard Monte's voice saying what number he'd reached and suggesting that he leave a message. He sighed and hung up.

Monte was probably asleep, like any sane, normal human would be. He didn't have to keep doctor's hours anymore.

Come to think of it, neither did Morgan. He should go to bed. Instead, however, he meandered over to his desk with his beer and took a seat. He flipped open his laptop and stretched his hands over the keyboard like a virtuoso getting ready to play a concert.

He felt like he was narrowing in on what might have been going on with the victims medically. He was nearly certain it had to be viral, not something genetic, but after ninety minutes, he still didn't have a definitive answer. There were just too damn many viruses and they all mutated too damn quickly. A virus, however, argued for something contagious. Could they both have caught something at the same place? He needed more information. Maybe they'd find that common point tomorrow at the community center.

He shut down the computer and took a swig of his now warm beer. He made a face and then went into the kitchen to pour it down the sink. He'd barely drunk half of it. The work had distracted him and made him feel much better than the booze could have ever done. He'd made some progress. He had a few avenues to explore, but they would wait for tomorrow, which would be coming all too soon.

CHAPTER TWELVE

Morgan belted himself into Danielle's vehicle the next morning. "Have we heard anything back from the Medical Examiner yet?"

"Good morning to you too." Danielle pointed to a second coffee in the cup holders. "Cream and no sugar, right?"

"Perfect." He sipped the coffee. "About the ME?"

"No. Nothing yet. Why?"

"I did some research last night. I'm struggling to find anything that would connect the jaundice, the lumps on the women's necks, and the rash, but I think it has to be something viral. I was hoping the autopsy report would give me some other avenues to go down."

"I'll let you know as soon as I know." Then she frowned. "You were researching last night? How late were you up?"

"Late enough." He shrugged.

She gave him a bit of side-eye. "Burnout is a real danger. Sleep when you can, Morgan."

He had to admit, she did look a lot more rested than she had the night before. He made a mental note to remind himself that he wasn't a resident anymore. Those punishing hours were behind him.

The Phillips Community Center was a modern three-story red brick building with few concrete details thrown in as a nod to the Federalist style that dominated so much of DC architecture. To one side, there was a fenced playground with a twisting slide, swings, a rock climbing wall, and a firefighter's pole. Everything was blue, green, or yellow and the ground was covered with a black rubbery material. Kids in shorts and matching t-shirts that read Phillips Preschool scampered across and around all of it.

Morgan's steps slowed. Was there anything better than the sound of children laughing?

Danielle looked over at him with one eyebrow arched. He pretended he didn't see and pushed open the doors of the community center, holding one open for her.

She gave him a quizzical look, but didn't press any further. She walked up to the reception desk. "We have an appointment with Anand Laghari."

56

The receptionist, a skinny Black girl with her hair done up in afro puffs, looked up at Danielle, head cocked to one side. "And you are?"

Danielle flipped out her badge. "Special Agent Danielle Hernandez. We have an appointment." She stressed the last word as she repeated it.

The girl sat up straighter, eyes bright. "FBI? Legit?"

Danielle laughed. "100 percent legit."

"You got a gun?" she asked.

Danielle didn't answer.

The girl pointed to Morgan. "And him?"

"A consultant," he said.

She barely acknowledged Morgan, staying focused on Danielle. "So, you're the boss."

"100 percent," Morgan said.

The girl laughed. "Awesome! I'll call Anand. He'll be right out. You can wait over there." She pointed to a bright blue foam couch that had seen better days. They walked over to it, but neither of them sat.

Minutes later, an east Asian man, most likely Indian, came out of the back. He had dark skin, hair, and eyes. He wore khakis and a Polo shirt, and his stomach protruded a bit over his belt. "Agent Hernandez. Dr. Stark. Come on back. Sorry to keep you waiting."

"No problem."

They followed Laghari down a hall lined with what looked like classrooms to Morgan, each with a window and a door. Peeking inside as they walked by, he could see chairs set up in rows facing a whiteboard at the front of most rooms. Except one. That one had the chairs set up in a circle. The carpet was utilitarian, but clean. The walls held posters advertising events that had been held at the center.

What had Kimberly and Angelica been doing here every Thursday night?

Laghari turned at the end of the hall and entered the first room on his right. The office was a study in controlled chaos. Everywhere Morgan looked there was some kind of colorful artwork and the desk was covered with papers and catalogs.

Laghari sat down behind the desk and gestured to the two chairs opposite him for Morgan and Danielle.

"So, how can I help you?"

"We were hoping to find out what classes or groups meet here at the community center on Thursday evenings," Danielle said, cutting right to the chase.

"Classes? None at the moment. We've got a hiatus going through the summer so we can focus on our enrichment activities for the kids.

So many of them have no place to go during the summer months." He gestured vaguely in the direction of the playground, then opened a file on his computer. "Oh. We do have one group that meets here year-round on Thursdays."

"What's that?" Morgan leaned forward, anxious to hear if whatever group met here might start them in a direction that could help them find Angelica's and Kimberly's killer. Some kind of class or support group might be the hint he needed to help him narrow down what was going on medically with the two women.

"Anger management."

That couldn't be right. Nothing they'd seen in either woman's profiles or heard from their families made it seem like either would need help with anger management. "You're sure that's the only group?"

Laghari nodded.

Morgan looked over at Danielle who looked equally as perplexed. She'd pulled her ponytail over one shoulder and was tugging on the end of it. "Do people have to register for this meeting?"

"Not exactly. Most are referred here. Some by therapists." He slid his glasses down his nose to look at them over the rim. "Some by law enforcement."

Morgan's pulse quickened. They were onto something. He could feel it.

"They have to show ID and sign in," Laghari said. "To prove they attended."

Of course. If it was part of someone's sentencing that they attend anger management classes, they'd have to show proof that they had actually done so.

"Could we see those lists?" Danielle asked, scooting forward on her chair, a sure sign that she felt the same way that Morgan did. This was their break. This was the moment the case would split wide open.

Laghari rubbed his chin. "I don't think so. I think that violates a lot of privacy rules."

Danielle's jaw hardened. "Mr. Laghari, I understand you wanting to safeguard people's privacy, but we're investigating two murders here. I think that probably supersedes any privacy rules in place about your attendance sheets."

Laghari's eyes went wide. "Murder? Someone was murdered?"

"Murders," Morgan corrected. "Two women are dead. It's possible that they have a connection with this anger management group."

Laghari slumped back in his chair and let his head fall back. "Let me call Lisa. She's the one who runs the group. She'll know the rules about what we can and can't release better than I do. Plus, she's the one with the lists." He took out his cell phone, hit a few buttons, and then held the phone to his ear. "Yeah. Lisa? Do you have a minute? Could you come to my office?"

A pause.

"Yes. Now."

He hung up. "She's on her way."

Morgan felt like he was going to jump out of his skin. He looked over at Danielle who had sat back in her chair and was checking her phone. How did she stay so cool? Then he noticed how one index finger was tapping out a rhythm on her thigh. The cool was an act. A good one, but not perfect. She had a tell.

"I can't believe this is happening," Laghari said, shaking his head. "Murders. Linked to one of our groups." His face had gone ashen.

Morgan mentally crossed him off any kind of suspect list. Unless he was an Oscar-worthy actor, he hadn't known that the murders of Kimberly Samson and Angelica McNally were in any way connected to his community center, if he even knew about them at all.

A sweet looking white woman who Morgan pegged as being in her early sixties came in. She had on a turquoise tank top with a ruffled neck and a knee-length skirt. Her white hair was styled in a layered bob that framed her face in a way that made it clear that the woman had been quite a looker in her younger days.

"Anand, what is it?" She stopped in the doorway taking in all three people, but then focusing back on Laghari. "Are you okay? You don't look well."

Laghari swallowed hard. "I think I'm a bit in shock. You should sit down too."

Without questioning him, but with a curious look at Morgan and Danielle, Lisa pulled a chair out from against the wall. "What's going on?"

Laghari gestured at Danielle to explain.

"Two women have been murdered in the past week in the same manner. The FBI thinks the murders might have been perpetrated by the same person. We're looking for a connection between the victims that might help us figure out who murdered them. We think that connection might be your Anger Management Group that meets on Thursdays."

Lisa froze. "My group? Here?"

"Yes, ma'am," Danielle said. "We were hoping to see the sign-in

59

sheets for your meetings so we could confirm that both victims were part of your group."

Lisa was shaking her head no before Danielle finished speaking. "I'm sorry. No. That's privileged. We don't release those names."

"Lisa," Laghari said. "We're talking about murders."

Lisa's face crumpled. "I understand that, but these people . . . If they think their privacy won't be respected, they won't come. How many more people might be murdered because someone was afraid others would find out that they attended anger management training? I wish I could help you, but no."

She had a point. There were so many reasons that respecting patient privacy was important. Morgan felt a clutch in his stomach. That was exactly the principle he'd violated at Georgetown. It was the reason he was on leave at the moment. He'd violated that sanctity. He dropped his head for a moment, but then he remembered why he'd done what he did. He'd done it to stop a murderer. Sometimes doing what was right meant not following the rules. Maybe there was a way around it here too.

"You run the group personally?" he asked.

Lisa nodded. "Yes."

"So you'd recognize anyone who attended it?" He glanced over at Danielle to see if she was following his reasoning. She nodded at him, giving him the go ahead to move forward.

"Absolutely. I try to make a personal connection with everyone who comes to the group, even if it's only once." Lisa smoothed her skirt over her knees.

"Could we show you photos of the two women? They're both deceased. If their murders are somehow tied to the group, I think you could make a very solid argument that there was no imminence of harm." The rules around patient privacy after death were complicated, but Morgan felt Lisa would be able to present a very reasonable hypothesis that identifying whether or not they were in the group wouldn't violate HIPAA regulations.

Lisa folded her hands in her lap and looked down at them. Morgan held his breath as he waited for her answer. Finally, she looked up at them. "I'll look at their photos."

Danielle threw a glance of gratitude Morgan's way then pulled a photo up on her cell phone and showed it to Lisa.

Lisa blinked a few times and sat back farther in her chair. "That's Kimberly," she said, her voice small. "She's dead? You're sure?"

"I'm so sorry," Danielle said. "But yes. We're sure."

"That poor woman," Lisa's brown eyes filled with tears. "You'd better show me the other one."

Danielle tapped on her screen to bring up the other photo and showed that one to Lisa.

Lisa's hand went over her mouth. "Angelica," she whispered. "Oh, no. Neither of them was here last night. I didn't think anything of it. Their attendance isn't court-mandated. They can attend or not. It's up to them." She stopped herself. "It was up to them."

The tears spilled over Lisa's eyes and Laghari handed her a box of tissues. Danielle gave Lisa a few moments to collect herself. "Was there anyone else who wasn't there last night? Someone who usually comes to the group, but hasn't been recently?"

Lisa shook her head. "I'm not sure."

"We'd like to see the sign-in sheets for the group for the past few months," Danielle said.

Lisa's head shot up. "Oh, no. I couldn't do that."

Danielle's jaw tightened. "We can get a subpoena for it."

Lisa looked over at Laghari. He thought for a moment and then nodded at her. "I think we should cooperate, Lisa. There's clearly a connection. We have to do everything we can to help before anyone else gets hurt."

Lisa's head dropped. "You're right. I know you are." Then she stood. "Come with me to my office."

"Thank you, Mr. Laghari," Danielle said as she stood, straightening her pant legs.

Morgan stood as well and reached over to shake the man's hand. "We appreciate your cooperation."

Laghari took his hand. "I took on this kind of work to help my community. Not helping you protect people who were coming here to better themselves goes against all of what I believe in. I'm just hoping you can respect the people who might not have had anything to do with this tragedy."

"We'll do our best," Morgan assured him and then followed the two women out of the room.

Lisa led them down another corridor to a room that looked much less business-like than Laghari's office. No desk. Just an overstuffed armchair across from a couch. A low coffee table stood between them with a box of tissues on it. "Have a seat," she said as she hurried over to a set of horizontal files that looked more like a credenza than office furniture.

Morgan sat, but Danielle stayed standing, nearly quivering with nervous energy.

Lisa pulled out a clipboard that had several sheets of paper on it. "How far back would you like me to go?"

Danielle squinted as she thought for a moment and then asked, "How long have Kimberly and Angelica been attending the group."

Lisa frowned and flipped through the pages. "I think about three months."

"Then that's what we need."

"I'll make copies for you." Lisa left the office.

"What do you think?" Morgan asked.

Danielle paced the small room. "Too soon to tell, but it feels like the best lead we've had so far. It's an actual connection between the two women while they were still alive, which we haven't had before."

That was true, but anger management? It simply didn't make sense to Morgan. Maybe he was wrong. Maybe the rash was a coincidence. It seemed like an awfully big one. If the connection between the two women ended up not being medical, would he be able to help Danielle at all? Could the community center be the point of contagion for whatever virus the women had picked up? He hadn't seen anyone else on the premises with similar symptoms. Maybe that would bear some more investigation.

Lisa came back into the room and handed Danielle a file folder. "Here they are."

"Thank you. We appreciate your cooperation." Danielle went to take the file, but Lisa held onto it for a moment before releasing it.

"I know you're looking for a murderer, but all these people are fragile in their own ways. People don't get angry for no reason. There's something in their past, something that's been done to them, that makes them that way. I hope you'll be compassionate."

Danielle looked Lisa in the eyes. "I will do my best."

"See that you do."

And with that, Morgan and Danielle left the room.

CHAPTER THIRTEEN

At the car, Danielle flipped open the file folder on the hood and took out her phone.

"What are you doing?"

"I'm going to take some photos and send these to Divinia and Henry to get started on background checks. By the time we get to the office, they'll have some of them done."

"Smart." Morgan held down the pages so they didn't drift in the slight summer breeze. The sheets had names, phone numbers, and addresses.

Once she was done snapping photos, Danielle called the office. "I'm sending you some sign-in sheets. I'd like background checks on as many of the people listed as possible. You should have enough information here."

She hung up and fired off a text with the photos attached.

They got in the car, and Danielle started the engine. Morgan angled the vents so the air conditioner would blow onto his face. The few minutes it had taken to take the photos of the sign-in sheets had left him feeling damp and wilted. "Here's what I don't understand. Why are our victims attending an anger management group?" he asked.

Danielle shook her head and drove out of the parking lot. "No idea. Nothing in either woman's background check showed anything that points in that direction. Maybe as we dig further we'll find something, but I'm as surprised as you are."

Returning to the FBI building, they made their way back to the conference room, stopping first at the guard desk as always.

"Oh, Dr. Stark," the guard said. "Here you go." She handed him a badge on a lanyard.

He looked down at it. Over the years, he'd had plenty of badges. Every hospital he'd ever worked in required staff to wear them and they often had to use them to get in and out of certain areas. This one felt different, though. It didn't feel like just another badge. It felt important. "Thanks, Marilyn." He looped it over his head to let it dangle at his chest.

"Looks good on you," she said. "Now go catch those bad guys."

63

Morgan gave her a salute, and then walked to the elevator and pushed the button for the fifth floor. Danielle's phone pinged.

"Looks like we've got good timing. Henry says they're finished running background checks on the names we sent them."

When they got to Danielle's unit, Morgan held up a hand and used his badge to unlock the door, which he then held open for Danielle.

In the conference room, Henry and Divinia had tacked information about the community center and the anger management group onto the whiteboards.

"So what do you have on the attendees?" Danielle asked.

"Unfortunately, mainly a great big nothing," Divinia said. "Some speeding tickets, a couple of people with more credit card debt than they can reasonably handle, a divorce or two, but nothing criminal."

"Nothing?" Morgan sank down in a chair, suddenly undone by disappointment. He'd been sure they were onto something.

Danielle picked up the stack of paper and started looking through it, shaking her head. "There's some kind of connection here. I know it."

Divinia pursed her lips. "Don't a lot of people go into things like anger management classes to avoid having something on their records?"

"Sure," Danielle said. "It's a diversion thing, trying to keep people out of the system."

"So maybe we're not seeing everything here," Divinia said.

Danielle grimaced. "If they're not in the system, how do we find out who might have had an issue with Kimberly and Angelica?"

Henry was running his finger down the list of attendees at each meeting. "What if we look at men who have been attending the same meetings that Kimberly and Angelica attended, but weren't there Thursday night? It's one thing to walk away from a murder, but to go back to something as intimate as a support group, knowing that you'd murdered two of the usual attendees? That would take some pretty enormous balls."

"Good idea," Danielle said. "But that could take some time."

"On it," Divinia said, turning to her laptop. "I've been making a spreadsheet already. I should be able to sort it and do a search."

"Terrific." Danielle slumped down in one of the chairs and blew out a breath.

"Are there photos of any of the attendees?" Morgan asked, lowering himself into a chair as well.

"We've got driver's license photos for most of them," Henry said.

That wouldn't get him what he wanted. Not necessarily. He'd be better off with social media posts. He wanted recent candid photos, ones that might reveal a rash like Kimberly's and Angelica's or a lump or some of the telltale signs of jaundice. "How many people are we talking about?" Maybe he could start searching for them on his own.

"Around forty-five total," Divinia said, not looking up from her laptop.

That would take some time.

"Okay. I've got three men who were regulars that weren't at Thursday's meeting." Divinia hit a button and the printer whirred. She retrieved the papers and then stuck them on the whiteboard. "Meet Titus Hammett, Russ Chaffin, and Bryon Lundstrom."

Three white men. They all looked to be in their thirties or forties. Morgan got up and peered at the photos. No rashes that he could see. No lipomas, although Lundstrom and Hammett both had on dress shirts with ties. None of that would be visible. Chaffin had on a shirt with an open collar. Nothing visible there. Then again, who knew when those photos were taken.

"And nothing came up on background checks of any of them?" Danielle asked, getting up to join Morgan at the photos.

Henry rifled through some papers. "Lundstrom is getting divorced."

"Which doesn't make someone automatically murderous," Morgan said, feeling a little put upon. He was getting divorced and he wasn't going after anyone with a baseball bat.

Henry continued as if Morgan hadn't said anything, "Chaffin has a couple unpaid parking tickets, but nothing on Hammett."

"Where do these guys live and work?" Danielle looked at her watch. "I'd love to talk to all three of them. Let's start with Lundstrom."

"He's over in Brentwood," Divinia said.

Morgan glanced at the map. Brentwood wasn't too far from the pushpins Henry had put in the map marking where Angelica and Kimberly had been killed. They were definitely in this guy's comfort zone.

"Where does he work?" Danielle asked, gathering up her jacket.

Henry looked up. "He's an Assistant Manager at a big sporting goods store."

Morgan's head shot up. "The kind of store that would sell baseball bats?"

Danielle's jaw clenched. "Let's go have a chat with Mr. Lundstrom."

CHAPTER FOURTEEN

Morgan got out of the SUV in front of Accent Sports Equipment and let out a low whistle. "This place is huge."

It was easily three stories high with a giant sign proclaiming its name.

"I've heard they have batting cages and some virtual reality golf bays." Danielle walked over to stand next to him, hands on hips.

"I had no idea." Morgan shook his head.

"Maybe you need to get out of the hospital more." Danielle started for the front door.

"That won't be a problem for the next few months." Morgan fell in step next to her.

"Your hearing went that well, huh?" The sliding doors whooshed open at her approach. "I hadn't wanted to ask."

Morgan didn't much want to tell. Luckily, the customer service desk was right inside the doors and he was spared from having to give Danielle the gory details.

"We'd like to talk to Mr. Lundstrom," Danielle told the young man behind the desk. He was a good-looking kid. Probably no more than twenty with jet black hair and deep, dark brown eyes marked by an epicanthal fold. His name tag read Zachary.

"Do you have an appointment?" he asked.

"No, but he'll want to talk to us." Danielle leaned her elbows onto the high counter.

Zach shook his head. "I'm sorry, but you have to have an appointment to go to the executive offices."

Danielle sighed and pulled out her badge. "How about you call Mr. Lundstrom and tell him the FBI is here to ask him some questions. I'm betting he'll be happy to have us come up and speak to him in private."

Young Zach's eyes got very big. "Yes, ma'am. Right away."

Morgan turned to take in the whole place. It was overwhelming. Everywhere he looked there were neon signs flashing and the noise of bats cracking against baseballs and clubs thunking against balls. "So everything here is virtual?" he asked.

Danielle cocked her head to one side. "I think the games you play here are, but you can buy actual equipment."

Morgan knew they were both thinking about the baseball bat.

Lundstrom came hurrying toward them from across the floor. Morgan grimaced. He still had on a dress shirt with a tie. No way could he see any of the possible symptoms that Angelica and Kimberly had. He squinted to see if there was any yellowing of the whites of Lundstrom's eyes, but he couldn't see any.

"I'm Bryon Lundstrom. Can I help you?" he said when he reached them.

Danielle showed him her badge. "Could we speak somewhere private?"

He nodded vigorously. "Follow me."

He led them back through a locked door into a suite of offices. "We can talk in my office." He gestured for them to follow him into a room on the right.

Lundstrom sat down behind his desk and gestured to the guest chairs across from him. "How can I help the FBI?" His voice was hearty, but he licked his lips and Morgan saw a slight twitch in the man's right eye. He was nervous.

"Could you tell me where you were on Sunday night between 9 p.m. and 2 a.m. and on Thursday morning between 1 a.m. and 3 a.m.?" Danielle pulled out her notebook.

"Of this week?" Lundstrom asked, then held up his hand. "Never mind. It doesn't matter. The answer would be the same for this week, last week, and the week before. I was home. With my family." He gestured to a photo behind him of himself with a dark-haired woman and two girls.

"Can anyone vouch for that?" Danielle asked, pencil poised over paper.

Morgan watched Lundstrom's face for any sign of distress. What he read there was much closer to confusion.

"My wife," Lundstrom said slowly, still appearing nonplussed.

"Would she have been awake during that time?" Danielle jotted something down.

Lundstrom's head drooped and then came back up. "We were both up on Thursday morning. Jenny caught some kind of bug. Threw up all over her bed. We were up from midnight until about two in the morning, cleaning her up, changing the sheets, and getting her settled."

"May I have your wife's phone number, please?" Danielle asked.

Lundstrom jotted some numbers down on the back of a business card and pushed it across the desk to Danielle. "Now, can I ask what all

67

this is about?"

"Mr. Lundstrom, do you know Kimberly Samson and Angelica McNally?" Danielle pulled out photos of the two women and put them on his desk.

Lundstrom got a little pale. "Yes. I know both those women. Why?"

"They were both murdered this week," Danielle said, with no inflection in her voice.

Morgan recognized the technique. He'd used it when having to deliver bad news to a family. There was no need to ratchet up the tension, so you kept your own voice calm and well-modulated.

"No. I heard something on the news about some murders, but I had no idea it was Kimberly and Angelica." He slid the photos closer to himself. "Those poor girls."

Poor girls, indeed.

"We know you attended an anger management group with them," Danielle said. "Is there a reason you weren't there on Thursday night?"

Lundstrom held out his hands palms up. "I was exhausted from being up half the night with Jenny. I went home and crashed." He looked back and forth between Morgan and Danielle. "You think this has something to do with the group?"

"We're not sure yet, but it does seem to be a big coincidence that they attended the same anger management group and were murdered within a couple of days of each other." Danielle leaned back and crossed her legs. "Is there anybody at the anger management group that paid particular attention to Kimberly or Angelica or both? The attention doesn't have to have been negative."

Lundstrom sighed, "Russ Chaffin."

Danielle sat up straighter. Chaffin was one of the names that Divinia had mentioned. He was one of the three men who hadn't been at the group meeting on Thursday. "Tell me about him, about what he did around Kimberly and Angelica."

Lundstrom scrubbed his hand across his face. "Most of the people in our group are men. Lisa explained to us that men may not be any angrier than women, but we do express it differently. We tend to be more physical and more impulsive. That made Kimberly and Angelica more noticeable."

"And Chaffin definitely noticed?" Morgan asked, leaning forward with his forearms braced on his knees.

"Yes. Very obviously. He was . . . taken with first Kimberly and then later with Angelica." Lundstrom made a face as if he didn't quite approve.

"How did he show being taken with them?" Danielle asked.

"He made a point of sitting next to them, chatting with them during social time beforehand and afterwards, and then when they weren't around," Lundstrom paused and then drew a deep breath and went on, "I heard him making comments to some of the other men."

"What kind of comments?" Morgan asked.

A little bit of red crept up Lundstrom's cheeks. Whatever Chaffin had done, Lundstrom definitely didn't approve. "Creepy. Lewd."

"Can you be more specific?" Danielle pressed.

Another sigh. Lundstrom was clearly not happy about sharing any of it. "One time, after Angelica got up and left the room, Chaffin leaned over and sniffed her chair and then made these smacking noises with his lips. Some of the men laughed."

Danielle made a face. "What did you do?"

"Nothing. I didn't want to be any part of it. I think Lisa might have heard, though. She spent a lot of time talking about micro-aggressions, specifically sexual ones, that night."

Danielle stood. "Thank you, Mr. Lundstrom. You've been very helpful."

He stood, but Danielle waved him away. "We can see ourselves out."

She pulled out her phone as they walked out of the store. "Henry, I need an address for Russ Chaffin."

She listened for a moment and then put her phone back in her pocket, a slightly sick look on her face. "Chaffin is a PE Coach at a high school. He coaches the girls' Lacrosse team."

Morgan felt a little sick thinking about a man like that around young women.

"School's not out for two more hours. How about we go pay a visit to Coach Chaffin?"

CHAPTER FIFTEEN

The ride to the high school where Russ Chaffin taught and coached wasn't going to be a long one. Morgan wanted to be prepared when they arrived.

"So what will we do when we get there?" Morgan asked. "Good cop, bad cop again?"

"Play it as it lays," Danielle said. "How Chaffin reacts will dictate a lot of how we act. Let's hope he plays it cool."

"And if he doesn't?" Smithson hadn't put up much of a fight, but who knew what they would face with Chaffin?

"I'll deal with it." She slid her sunglasses down to look over them at Morgan. "Just me. Right? No heroics from you, okay?"

Morgan held his hands up in front of himself. "No heroics from me. I promise. I've learned my lesson."

She made a funny noise in the back of her throat. "I hope so. For both of our sakes. The paperwork for injured consultants is huge and I really hate paperwork."

Morgan laughed. "You know I was always just trying to help, right?"

Danielle's face stilled. "I do know and I appreciate it. We just need to find a way for you to help that keeps you safe."

Morgan settled back in his seat. He'd made a few too many attempts to "help" Danielle during their last case together. She'd been justifiably angry with him and had even thrown him off the case altogether at one point. He'd seen the error of his ways, though. Danielle was more than capable of taking care of herself. The type of help she needed from him had nothing to do with running down and subduing bad guys.

She needed his powers of observation and his medical knowledge.

They pulled into the parking lot of the high school. Over on the field, they could see a group of girls with Lacrosse sticks lined up halfway down the field from the goal. One after the other, they'd scoop a ball up off the ground with a stick, run to an orange cone set up midway and to the left of the goal, do a spin turn, and run to a second cone set up in front of the goal, where they'd shoot.

70

A man wearing a baseball cap called out, "Good one, Jessie! Keep it up!" Morgan recognized him from the photo that Henry had found of Chaffin.

Chaffin put his hand up to his mouth for a moment and then slipped it back into his pocket. Then he turned to another man standing next to him and quietly said something. That man made a notation on the clipboard he was holding.

Danielle approached the man in the baseball cap. "Russ Chaffin?"

Chaffin turned and looked at her, letting his gaze roam up and down her body, before saying, "Who's asking?"

Morgan had some doubts as to whether or not Lisa's work on toning down the man's sexual aggression had been effective. He felt his own anger rising at the man's blatant leering and took a step forward, then tried to calm himself. Danielle would have this handled. She'd let him know if she needed or wanted help.

Danielle pulled out her badge and said, "FBI."

Chaffin barely hesitated. He waited one second. Maybe two. Then he took off running toward another parking lot on the far side of the field, most likely for faculty. Danielle started to take off after him, but Morgan put a hand on her arm. In this case, his medical knowledge might help with catching and subduing a suspect. "Don't go all out. He's not going to get far."

She gave him a funny look, but waited. "Why?"

"Asthma. He was using his inhaler as we walked up." As humid as it was, it would only make the man's asthma worse. Humidity makes the air move around less and eventually become stagnant. Stagnant air is full of all kinds of irritants that can set off an asthma attack. Clearly, the man had already been having some issues since he'd just used that inhaler. Running wasn't going to help.

"Thanks for the tip." She followed Chaffin at a slow jog and, sure enough, Chaffin's steps slowed when he was halfway across the field. He'd barely made it to the far edge of the field when Danielle caught up. He was already bent forward, hands braced on his thighs, trying to catch his breath. Danielle snapped cuffs on him and frogmarched him back across the field as the girls stared gape-mouthed from what had happened.

Morgan exchanged a glance with the other man, the one with the clipboard. "I think you're in charge of practice now." He walked back to the car to meet Danielle and their latest suspect.

He couldn't wait to hear what this one had to say for himself.

CHAPTER SIXTEEN

The man whistled to himself as he walked up the sunlit pathway through the azaleas. The red splotches of the flowers looked like the spray of blood he'd left in the secluded grotto where he'd met Sandra Cartmill for a picnic. The thought made him smile. It's amazing that there was such a lovely, lonely spot in the middle of Washington DC.

He hitched the yoga mat carrier up on his shoulder. It didn't, of course, hold a yoga mat. No, it had the bloody baseball bat that he'd used to stop Sandra for good. It also had his bloody clothes.

He'd learned with Kimberly how much blood there'd be. That had been a bit of a surprise. What a mess! Thank goodness he'd only needed to slide out her back door and into the dark alley where his car had been parked. He'd been better prepared with Angelica. He'd known that he'd get messy and had brought a change of clothes and some wet wipes to clean off the obvious evidence of what he'd done. He was even better prepared with Sandra.

He was getting good at this, and he was only going to get better. With each kill, he grew stronger and smarter. He wasn't going to get caught by something like blood spray on his clothes.

Oh, he wouldn't withstand a serious inspection of his body and clothes at the moment, but he didn't have to. Everybody saw what they wanted to see. A pleasant-looking white guy in his early thirties who had just finished up one of the afternoon yoga classes held in the Grove of State Trees.

Idiots. All of them.

Not him, though, of course. He wasn't an idiot. Oh, no, he was smarter than all of them, even if they didn't seem to understand that.

He'd gotten away with murder twice already, and with Sandra dispatched, it would be three times.

Three dead women and not so much as a discreet inquiry about him, who he was, or where he'd been. No photos of him on the news. No composite sketches. No description of his car.

It was just more proof as to how much better he was than all of them.

The thought gave him such satisfaction that he actually laughed out loud. When was the last time he'd done that? Weeks, easily. Maybe even a month. Certainly not since she'd broken up with him.

The happy buoyant feeling quickly soured, as he remembered why he was doing this. He was better than all of the rest of them, so why had she forsaken him? Why had she rejected him? These women would have had him. Why wouldn't she? They'd had the exact same disease as she had. She'd said that was why they had to break up, that was why she wouldn't see him anymore. It was wrong. She was wrong. They could have still been together.

He was clearly superior to most of the men on that stupid app she used. All three of those women had been clamoring to meet him. There was no reason for her not to want him, to have stopped wanting him.

But she hadn't wanted him. She'd looked him in the eye and told him it was over. She'd even told him that she'd cheated on him. That was how she'd gotten the stupid virus in the first place.

At the time, he'd been speechless. It was like being in an elevator that suddenly went into freefall. The bottom dropped out. He'd been crushed. He'd spent weeks moping. Then he'd done a little snooping. It wasn't stalking. Not really. He'd just wanted to see her, to watch the way she tucked her hair behind her ear, the way she skipped a little as she walked.

Instead, he'd gotten to the park outside her apartment just in time to see her kiss some guy in the doorway. She'd even done that thing where she lifted one foot up behind her. Then she'd opened the door and let the guy come in with her.

He knew what that meant. He knew exactly what that meant. It hadn't been that long ago that he was that guy, that he was the one that made her foot pop up.

That was when he got mad. Really mad. What the hell was she doing? For that matter, who was she to reject him? She was the one with the disease. She should have been begging him to stay.

He hadn't known what to do with his anger. It had swamped him, overwhelmed him, made him want to howl at the moon like a wolf. He'd gone searching online and found her on the app, flirting away with all those losers. He was so angry that he wanted to smash things. He wanted to smash her. Those thoughts were the ones that had scared him.

He loved her. He couldn't hurt her. He needed to find another way. He'd thought he could work it out of his system by dispatching these women who had so much in common with her. He just needed a way to blow off some steam, to take the temperature of his rage down. It had

73

worked for a bit too, but that feeling of satisfaction faded quicker with each one. He wasn't even back to the parking lot yet and he was already back to the crushing hurt of rejection that he'd felt when she'd dumped him.

There was apparently only so much gratification to be had when dealing with these stand-ins.

That was her fault too. Everywhere he turned, she was there taking things away from him.

Well, that was going to stop, and it was going to stop soon.

Her turn was coming.

Behind him, he heard someone scream.

CHAPTER SEVENTEEN

"Where are you taking me?" Chaffin demanded from the back seat of the car.

Morgan opened his mouth to answer, but Danielle tapped his thigh with one finger and gave a tiny shake of her head. Morgan sat back and shut his mouth.

"I have rights, you know. I want to know where you're taking me and why." Chaffin strained forward against the seat belt that Danielle had fastened around him.

Danielle didn't even glance over her shoulder at him.

"I will have your badge," he bellowed.

At that, Danielle allowed a small smile to quirk at her lips, but still said nothing. Morgan wasn't sure how she stayed so calm.

By the time they reached headquarters, Chaffin had burned himself out or at least had opted to fume silently. Danielle turned him over to Henry who met them at the garage. "You know where to put him." Those were the first words she'd spoken since they'd gotten in the car.

As Morgan and Danielle made their way to the unit, he asked, "Are we going to do good cop/bad cop again?"

Danielle stretched and loosened her neck like an athlete getting ready for a competition. "No, my friend. We're going 100 percent bad cop on this jerk."

Morgan looked over at her, at the way she marched up the stairs like a soldier going into battle.

She raised a hand to stop him before he said anything. "I played sports all throughout high school and college. I'm all too familiar with guys like him. Either he thinks he's superior to everyone else and will be over-confident. Or he wants to be superior and knows he's not and that's opened a deep well of insecurity in him. Either way, he's going to have a big problem with a woman taking control of the situation. I don't want him to think anyone is on his side, especially not another man." They got up to the unit.

"He's in room three," Henry told her.

"Thanks." Danielle picked up a stack of folders and walked down the hall. She banged into the interrogation room with Morgan behind

75

her. They sat down across from Chaffin whose hands remained cuffed and now clipped to the bar at the center of the table. A bead of sweat trickled down from his sideburns. His face was red, and he breathed heavily. Morgan hoped he didn't have a heart attack or an asthma attack right there in the interrogation room.

Danielle pulled the photos of Angelica and Kimberly when they were still alive out of her file folders and slammed them down in front of Chaffin. "Mr. Chaffin, do you know these women?"

Chaffin looked from one photo to the other and up at Danielle, then he looked over at Morgan. "Why? What's this about?"

Danielle snapped her fingers in front of his face. "Over here, Chaffin. I'm asking the questions."

His eyes narrowed and he opened his mouth as if he was going to start yelling, but then apparently thought better of it. "Yes. I know them."

"How did you meet them?" She shot the question at him almost before he was done answering.

Chaffin pushed back in his chair, as if he could back away from the whole situation, but it only made it so he had to bend at the waist because of the way his wrists were cuffed. "I'd rather not say."

"Oh, would you prefer not to talk?" Danielle's voice had gone singsong and mocking. Chaffin's chin began to quiver. "Well, too bad. You can tell me now, or I can arrest you and you can tell me all about it after you spend a night in lock-up."

Chaffin looked over at Morgan again who crossed his arms over his chest and did his best to look angry, but kept his mouth firmly shut.

"From my support group," Chaffin blurted out, his eyes wide enough that Morgan could see the white around the irises. "At the community center."

Danielle sat back in her chair, took a deep breath, and let it out. Then she crossed her arms and legs. "Better," she said as if Chaffin was performing for her. "What support group is that?"

"Anger management," Chaffin mumbled, looking down at the table. He bounced his knee.

"What's that?" Danielle cupped a hand behind her ear. "I didn't hear you. You're going to need to speak up."

Chaffin lifted his head. "They go to my anger management support group. They're new. They've only been to a couple of sessions. I barely know them." The knee bounced faster.

He was referring to the women in the present tense. Did he not know they were dead? Morgan glanced over at Danielle. Had she

76

caught that?

"When was the last time you saw either one of these women?" Danielle asked.

Chaffin frowned. "I wasn't at the last meeting. They were both at the meeting before that I think." He shrugged. "It's not for everybody. It helps some people more than others."

"Are you one of the people it helps, Mr. Chaffin?"

He nodded vigorously. "Absolutely. I've been much better at controlling outbursts and I haven't thrown, smashed, or broken anything in months."

Morgan cringed. He'd been known to have a temper when he was trying to protect his patients, but it sounded like this guy flew out of control for no good reason. Smashing things? Breaking things? It sounded like a toddler having tantrum.

Danielle sat upright. "You smash things, Chaffin? Break them? You ever use a baseball bat?"

His brows drew down and he looked sincerely confused. "Baseball bat? No. I'm a Lacrosse coach."

Danielle snorted. "I didn't ask for your resumé. I asked if you smashed things with a baseball bat."

"No." There was a sarcastic tinge to his answer.

Danielle narrowed her eyes at him. "Do you own a baseball bat?" she pressed.

"No."

"You sure about that? If we get a search warrant for your house, we're not going to find any baseball bats?" Danielle leaned forward now, getting into Chaffin's space.

Chaffin looked back and forth between Danielle and Morgan. "Search warrant? Why would you get a search warrant for my house? What's all this about a baseball bat? What's going on here?"

"Where were you on Sunday and Thursday nights?" Danielle asked. "Between 7 p.m. and 2 a.m.?"

"I don't know. I'd have to check my calendar." He was trying to sound tough, but Morgan could see the confusion and fear creeping up on him.

"How about you just think hard?" Danielle jutted her chin at him.

Chaffin looked down at his hands and then his head shot up. "I was with the girls' Lacrosse team in Pittsburgh. We left last Friday and were there for a weekend of clinics and drills and then there was a mini tournament." The knee was going at supersonic speeds now.

"Will anybody be able to corroborate that?"

"Yeah. Like about eighty people. The folks that were running the clinics, the other coaches, my players." Chaffin was warming to his topic, sitting up straighter and jutting his chest out.

Pittsburgh was at least four hours away from DC. It would be damn hard for Chaffin to get back to DC, commit a brutal murder, and then return without his absence being noticed by someone. To have done it twice? It seemed pretty much impossible.

Someone tapped at the door and it opened. Henry stuck his head in. "Need to talk to you, boss."

Danielle nodded and then stood. "I'll be right back."

Morgan and Chaffin sat. The artificial light of the interrogation room reflected off the scarred metal table with its iron bar.

Morgan contemplated the man before him. Maybe they weren't playing good cop/bad cop, but it seemed like a decent time to try to establish some of that rapport that Danielle had said was helpful. It wasn't like he didn't know how to do it. Morgan had been dealing with people who were often having some of the worst days of their lives for years now. He'd dealt with difficult before. "How long have you had asthma?" he asked.

"My whole life." Chaffin shrugged and looked away.

Okay. No connection that way. Try another tactic. That was part of the skill set. If one avenue of inquiry shut down, you tried another one. "How'd you end up in anger management treatment?"

Chaffin looked back at him, eyes squinted in suspicion. "Why?"

Morgan lifted his hands in a "why not" gesture. "Not much else to do besides chat right now."

Chaffin slumped back in the chair again. "Mandated by the school district."

Interesting. "Does everyone have to do it?"

Chaffin shook his head. "No. Just special people like me."

Morgan chuckled at the attempt at a joke. Showing that you both found the same things funny was a way of establishing that you were all on the same team. "How'd you show 'em you were so special?"

Chaffin rubbed at his knuckles. "Had a disagreement with the Athletic Director. It got a little heated." His head came up again, eyes blazing. "It was just passionate talk. I don't know why she had to go and report me to the Superintendent. It's bullshit."

Ah, interesting. Danielle had been right. The guy clearly had a problem with women. Was it enough of a problem to create the kind of rage that had been behind the attacks on Kimberly and Angelica? Morgan wasn't sure. Before Morgan could comment, Danielle returned.

"Mr. Chaffin, you're free to go." She unlocked his handcuffs from the bar in the middle of the table.

Chaffin rubbed his wrists as if they'd been chafed, although Morgan was certain Danielle had been quite careful to not tighten them too much. They'd been more for intimidation than for restraining the man. Chaffin stood. "What now?"

"We'll have an agent take you back to your school." Danielle picked up her stack of file folders and tapped them into a neat pile.

Chaffin didn't move. "Do I get some kind of apology?"

Danielle's eyebrows went up. "For what?"

"For humiliating me in front of my players! For making me look like a criminal!"

Danielle didn't say anything for a minute. She put one hand down on the back of a chair and leaned against it. She looked down at her shoes and then back up. "I think you trying to take off running was more what made you look like a criminal than anything we did. File it away under life lessons. If you run from law enforcement, we're going to think you have a reason."

Henry opened the door. "Come on, Mr. Chaffin. I'll give you a ride."

As Chaffin walked past Danielle, he muttered, "Bitch."

Morgan had had enough and moved to block the doorway. "How do your employers know how you're progressing in your anger management program?"

"Lisa gives them a weekly progress report."

"Mmhmm. And how do you think they'll feel if they get a report from law enforcement that your issues are far from resolved? And that you particularly should not be dealing with young women?"

Chiffon's eyes went wide and he stepped back. "What the hell?"

"You've got to admit, you've been pretty rude to Special Agent Hernandez here," Morgan said, his voice still calm, although he felt anything but. "She takes that kind of stuff in stride, but I tend to hold a grudge. How about you apologize?"

Chaffin looked as if steam might come out of his ears. "I'm sorry," he said to his shoes.

Morgan sighed. It was something, he supposed. He stepped out of the way to watch their one good lead walk out of the room.

"That wasn't necessary," Danielle said after Chaffin was gone.

"I know. He pissed me off, though."

Danielle snorted. "Maybe we should sign you up for anger management."

"Oh, I think I managed my anger just fine," Morgan replied. "So why are we letting him go?"

"His alibi checked out."

Before Danielle could say anything else, Divinia came into the room, her face drawn.

"What's wrong?" Danielle asked.

"There's been another victim."

CHAPTER EIGHTEEN

Morgan walked beside Danielle through the arboretum. It wasn't hard to pick out where they were going. A small crowd had gathered outside the crime scene tape.

Wondering if whoever was doing this would want to come back to watch the aftermath of his violence, Morgan scanned the faces. Would that be part of the thrill? Standing around watching law enforcement work with them none the wiser as to who he was or why he was doing this?

Danielle already had her badge out as they walked up to the young uniformed woman who was keeping people out. Sweat was running down the sides of her face. Morgan felt some sympathy for her. The air was thick and she was in the hot sun in a dark uniform with easily twenty-five or thirty pounds of equipment hanging off her utility belt.

She nodded at Danielle. "Sheehan is expecting you." She lifted the crime scene tape, and they ducked beneath it.

Sheehan was in short sleeves and jeans, but there were already sweat spots spreading beneath his arms. He'd been looking at something on the ground, but stood when he saw Danielle. "Special Agent Hernandez."

She smiled. "Detective Sheehan."

He was tall. Maybe even taller than Morgan. His hair was jet black and his skin was a light brown. His eyes were such a dark brown that Morgan almost couldn't make out the pupil.

"This is Dr. Morgan Stark. He's consulting on this case," Danielle gestured to Morgan.

He stuck out his hand and the two men shook. Sheehan's grip was firm, but he wasn't into that macho thing where a guy tries to crush another guy's hand.

"So, what do we have?" Danielle asked.

"Beyond the change in setting, it's nearly identical to McNally and Samson." Sheehan gestured for them to follow him.

The smell hit Morgan first. Even out here in the open, the smell of blood, injury, and death enveloped the area, magnified by the humidity in the air. They were standing by the remains of a young woman who

81

had been brutally beaten. Like Angelica and Kimberly, her face had been nearly obliterated. Morgan's heart sank. Senseless. Senseless and violent.

"Do you have an ID?" Danielle asked, walking carefully around the perimeter of the body.

"Got a wallet with a driver's license for Sandra Cartmill. We'll have to wait for fingerprints or DNA to be sure, though." He gestured to the young woman's ruined face.

Morgan looked down at the woman's hands, her arms sprawled out to either side of her. Through the blood, he could see the same rash that McNally and Smithson had had. She also had the same small lump on her neck. Her face was too ruined to see if there was a slight yellow cast to her sclera as well, but he'd bet his bottom dollar that she was jaundiced too. Her fingers curled inward. He froze. Then he crouched down to get a better look.

"What is it, Morgan?" Danielle asked.

"Can I touch her?" he asked.

"No!" Both Danielle and Sheehan shouted.

He pushed back and looked up at them. "Please."

Sheehan then crouched down next to him. "What do you need to see?"

"Her fingernails." Morgan's heart had sped up. He had it. He was nearly certain. A blood test would confirm it all, but he wanted to be sure he was seeing what he thought he was seeing.

Sheehan looked up at Danielle, a quizzical expression on his face. She made a rolling gesture with his hand. "Show him what he needs to see. Trust me. It'll be worth it."

Sheehan put on gloves and pulled a pen out of his pocket. Carefully, he bent Sandra Cartmill's fingers closer to her palms.

And there it was. The final puzzle piece that made the picture come together. There had been a constellation of symptoms that pointed in too many different directions for him to narrow in on one diagnosis. This symptom, however, made it all become clear.

"I know what connects all three of the victims," Morgan stood up. "Morris will have to confirm it with a blood test, but I'm pretty certain."

"Don't keep us in suspense, Morgan," Danielle said.

He shook his head. "I should have seen it sooner. It all makes sense."

"Morgan!" Danielle snapped.

"They all have Hecar Sinilus Inflammatorio or HSI. It's a sexually transmitted infection that causes rashes on the chest and abdomen, swollen lymph nodes in the neck, jaundice, and discoloration of the lunulae, those little half-moons on your fingernails," he blurted. He couldn't believe he hadn't connected the symptoms before: the lump on their necks, the rash, and the jaundice. But it was the slight green tinge to the woman's lunulae that brought it all home. HSI was a new strain of an old virus that had been making a resurgence, much to the chagrin of public health officials across the country, but particularly on the east coast.

Sheehan looked at him through narrowed eyes. "What the hell is HSI?"

"It's an STI." Morgan rubbed his face, the excitement of figuring out what it was already starting to ebb. "It can cause a build-up of copper in the liver and gallbladder that causes rashes, jaundice, and that slight greenish tinge at the base of her fingernails."

"How come I've never heard of it before?" Sheehan asked.

"Mainly because it hasn't really been a problem before. There was a very low level of transmission until recently." Morgan rubbed his jaw. He was glad to have figured out the medical connection, but he still wasn't sure how that was going to translate into finding the killer.

"Did the other women have the fingernail thing?" Danielle asked.

He shook his head. "I didn't check. I didn't think of it. We can call Morris, though. We have to anyway to have him run the right tests on McNally and Samson. He'll have to check for the specific antibodies."

"Is there a cure for it?" Sheehan asked.

"Unfortunately, no. The symptoms are manageable and certainly not fatal, but they're bothersome and, of course, no one wants to pass something like this on to other people." Another thought hit him. "It works with why they'd be at an anger management group too. People react in different ways. Sometimes they get pretty pissed off when they find out they have a chronic condition. They feel angry and betrayed. After all, someone they were intimate with gave it to them. Someone they trusted to get that close."

Danielle's took in a sharp breath. "Kimberly's mother mentioned a bad break-up with a boyfriend who cheated on her. Could the cheater have also given her HSI? That would definitely piss me off."

"Absolutely," Morgan said. "In general, though, women deal with a lot of guilt, embarrassment, and shame when they're diagnosed with an STI. They feel dirty and can strike out at others because of it. In the case of this particular disease, those psychological issues can be even worse than the actual disease. I've known a few doctors who've sent their patients with STIs to anger management for a time."

Danielle's index finger was doing its little tapping routine against her thigh. "And you wouldn't want to chat with your parents about it, either."

"Right. That would explain both women being cagey with their families about what they were doing with their Thursday nights." Morgan walked a few steps away from Sandra to take advantage of the shade of an oak tree.

Danielle and Sheehan walked over to join him. "You see why his input is so valuable?" Danielle said to Sheehan.

Sheehan held his hands up in front of himself. "I never doubted you for a moment."

She snorted. "Sure you didn't."

"The question is how does this help us? How do we proceed from here?" Sheehan rubbed the back of his neck.

Danielle sighed. "Therein lies the rub. It's not like we can do some kind of search for everybody with this STI. There's not going to be a database to search or search their medical records."

Morgan was well aware of that. It was breaking that rule that had him on leave from the hospital at the moment.

"We need to find another way to use this information," she said.

"Like what?" Sheehan asked.

She looked off into the distance and then suddenly straightened. "I've got a few ideas."

CHAPTER NINETEEN

Morgan opened the door to the SUV and got in. The air inside felt superheated. Once Danielle was settled behind the wheel, he asked, "So what are these plans?"

Danielle started the vehicle and Morgan closed his door. "Well, first we contact Morris to verify what you're thinking, and then we start doing some research of our own. I don't know anything about this disease. What can you tell me?" she asked.

"Honestly, not much. It's not something that I generally dealt with and this one wasn't even around when I was a resident. At least, it wasn't around in the form it's taken now." He'd glanced at the information about it when he'd been doing his research, but hadn't dug into the data.

Danielle made a face. "I don't understand what that means. What other form could it have taken?"

This he could explain. "Well, bacteria and viruses mutate, right?"

"Right. I've got that."

"So this particular infection has been around for decades, but didn't spread easily or rapidly. There was no reason to worry about it much. Then it acquired DNA from the virus that causes varicella." It was one of those really unlucky breaks that sometimes happened in public health. A virus that didn't spread easily suddenly merged with a virus that did, and a whole new set of problems appeared on the horizon.

"How the hell did it do that?" She glanced over at Morgan, clearly alarmed.

"I'm not sure you really want a lecture on genetic recombination, meiosis, and how chromosomes can fuse right now." He wasn't sure he wanted to give one either.

"Very astute of you, Dr. Stark. I do not."

He laughed. "I thought as much. The upshot is the recombination made it that much easier for HSI to spread. It's becoming a real problem." He'd seen a bulletin about it not that long ago. He should have thought of it sooner, although in his defense, he didn't see a lot of STIs in his practice. STIs are usually diagnosed and dealt with by people's primary care physicians. They generally didn't need the specialized high-level help that he provided for patients. Still, that cluster of symptoms isn't typical. He hoped that his slowness to reach a diagnosis didn't mean that they could have saved Sandra Cartmill. That would be devastating.

Danielle shook her head. "There's always something new to worry about."

"True enough."

They'd reached the FBI building and made their way back to the offices. Someone had added a third pushpin in the arboretum for Sandra Cartmill. The three murders made kind of a strange triangle that roughly bordered the Trinidad neighborhood. Would that help them zero in on the killer? Had they found the area he probably lived in? It was a fairly densely populated area, but he felt they were narrowing in on their suspect with every step they took.

"I'll call Morris," Morgan said and pulled out his phone. Damn it. He hadn't returned Ashley's call yet. He'd do it soon, but first things first.

The Medical Examiner answered on the second ring. Morgan was relieved. He didn't want to try to leave all he had to say in a voicemail.

"How can I help you, Dr. Stark?" Morris asked.

"Where are you on the McNally and Samson autopsies?"

"Finishing up now, actually. You were right about the jaundice, by the way. The lumps on the women's necks are harder to explain. They may just be very enlarged lymph nodes."

Yes. That made sense with a diagnosis of HSI. "What about the women's lunulae? Did you notice any discoloration?"

There was a sharp intake of breath. "How did you know that?"

Bingo. "I think it might be HSI. Can you test for that?"

"Now that I know what I'm testing for, absolutely." There was a pause. "That's not life threatening, though. How do you think it relates to the murders?"

"We're still not sure about that. There's a third victim coming your way. Sandra Cartmill. Can you be sure to test her for HSI antibodies too?"

"Will do." Then there was a pause. "A third victim. Is this guy escalating, Morgan? What are we in for here? Should we be warning the public?"

"I'm not sure. Right now, we're focusing on finding this man and stopping him before he kills again." Then it wouldn't matter if he was escalating or not.

"Good luck and let me know if there's anything more I can do to help," Morris said.

"Will do."

Morgan hung up. "He'll test all three victims for HSI. What have you found so far?"

"Not much," Danielle said, still tapping on her computer. "What's cymynazole?"

Morgan leaned over her shoulder to see one of those big "Ask Your Doctor About" ads that were the bane of most doctors' practices. "It's an anti-viral. They might be using it to control some of the symptoms of HSI, but it won't cure it. The best it can do is lighten the viral load."

"What good will that do?"

"Get the viral load low enough and the person won't have to worry about transmitting the virus to someone else. They've managed that with HIV. Not with HSI, though."

Danielle pushed back from the table. "The other things I'm seeing are mainly online coping classes. Even if we could get hold of the names of the people signing up for those classes, it'll be hell to figure out which ones are local. I'm worried we don't have that much more time before he strikes again."

Morgan's head started to throb. He needed to get away for a few minutes. "I'm going to take a break and think for a bit."

She nodded. "I'll keep plugging away here."

He stepped out into the hallway and hit the button for Ashley.

She answered immediately, "Hey, Morgan. How are you?"

He thought about it for a second before answering. How was he really? Excited. Absorbed. Focused. "Okay. You?"

"Are you sure? I know the hearing was . . . upsetting."

Morgan leaned against the wall and let his head fall back. The hearing should have been upsetting. He'd been too busy to really let it sink in. "I am sure. I've been distracted."

"Are you working with Danielle Hernandez still? Is that what's distracting you?" There was a weird tone in her voice.

"I'm helping with a case. I think we've had a big breakthrough on it, although we've yet to figure out how to leverage it. We will, though." They were going to catch this guy. The question was, could they do it before he killed again?

"Morgan, what are you doing?"

"What do you mean? I just said that I'm helping Danielle out on a case."

"You're not an FBI agent, Morgan. You're a doctor."

"Yeah, well, it's not like the medical establishment is making me feel welcome at the moment."

"That's temporary. They'll come to their senses."

He'd thought the same thing when Ashley had first told him she wanted a separation, that she'd realize how much he meant to her. It had been Morgan, who came to the realization of how much she meant to him, however, and as near as he could tell, he'd gotten there too late. "In the meantime, this is keeping me occupied."

"I suppose," she hesitated. "Is it keeping you occupied or is it keeping you obsessed?"

"Obsessed?" What was she talking about? He straightened up off the wall.

Ashley sighed. "You've spent your entire adult life focused on your career in medicine, often to the detriment of everything else in our life."

She didn't have to point out that their marriage was one of the things that suffered because of his focus. He'd done enough work to understand that. "Okay."

"Well, the second you're cut off from that career — and I do mean the very second — you find something else that you can put all your energies into. What about taking some time to figure out what it is and who it is you really want to be?"

She had a point about that. It had been something that had been in the back of his mind. He knew he was using the consulting gig with Danielle to keep from dealing with his feelings about being suspended. That wasn't all of it, though. Not by a long shot. "The person is killing young women."

Ashley hesitated. "So it's about your sister, then?"

Morgan rubbed a hand over his face. "Maybe. In a way. What if law enforcement had pulled out all the stops when she disappeared? What if they'd done literally everything? Including maybe pulling in civilian consultants? Maybe Fiona would be back with me." Maybe his parents wouldn't have died so young. Maybe he would have had the kind of balance in his life that would have kept him from putting up walls between Ashley and himself.

He heard voices in the background. "Just a second, Morgan."

He heard her speaking, but it was muffled. She'd clearly put her hand over the receiver. Then she was back. "I've got to go, Morgan. Call me later? We can talk more."

"Sure. We'll talk soon." He hung up feeling a little surge of hope in his chest. Ashley wanted him to check in. She wanted him to contact her. She wanted him to find some balance in his life. Maybe there was hope yet. Maybe it wasn't too late to salvage their marriage.

He'd been so lucky to meet her. It hadn't been easy back when he'd been in medical school. He was so busy. There'd been no time to date. Most of his fellow medical students had been using dating apps with pretty poor results. Then Ashley had walked into his life and taken his breath away.

He froze. All three of these women were single. Angelica was definitely looking to meet someone. Sandra had been at the arboretum, which was a regular place for people on first dates to go. Could they have been using a dating app? There were so many of them now, all specialized for different kinds of people. People over sixty, people from specific religions, farmers, people with tattoos, people looking to have affairs, and people looking for long-term relationships.

He threw open the door to the conference room and said, "Dating apps."

"Pardon me?" Danielle looked up from her computer.

"Is there a dating app for people with STIs?" He sat down next to her. "Or is there even one specifically for people with HSI?"

"Give me a second," Divinia said. "I'll look."

Morgan held his breath as Divinia tapped away on her computer. Then she said, "There definitely is. HSIPos."

Danielle frowned. "That seems fast. I'd never even heard of this STI and there's already a dating app specifically for people who have it?"

Divinia kept typing and then spent a few minutes reading what was on her screen. "So HSIPos is actually an offshoot of another dating app for people with STIs. They've got what's basically an umbrella program under which all of these other apps run. The infrastructure was there. It probably took a programmer less than a day to create the HSIPos offshoot."

Danielle did her double knock on the table and said, "Let's see if our victims are on it."

CHAPTER TWENTY

Morgan sat back, frustrated. It had taken Danielle about thirty minutes to find Kimberly Samson on HSIPos after Divinia confirmed that Kimberly had had the app on her phone. Angelica McNally had the app too. It was too soon to know if Sandra Cartmill did. They were still waiting for the subpoena for her phone information to go through.

That information was only so helpful, though. No one on the app used their real name. It was all usernames. Some cutesy. Some suggestive. Some Morgan had no explanation for.

"Found her!" Danielle said, pushing back from the table. She turned her laptop so Morgan could see Angelica McNally's photo at the top of her profile.

"CutiePie1024?" He squinted at her user name.

"Her birthday is October 24." Danielle turned the computer back to face her.

"How did you end up finding her?" There were so many people on the site. How did she narrow it down?

"I searched using a combination of age, gender, and geographical location, then combed through them from there."

"Are there a lot?" He'd known that the infection had been spreading, but hadn't done the math on what that meant for specific numbers in the population.

Danielle rubbed her eyes. "Hundreds. I need to figure out a way to narrow it down further. There's got to be a reason our unsub chose these specific women. Something more than what I've got so far."

Morgan looked at the two women's profiles, comparing what they'd put in them. "What does NOO mean? It looked like both Angelica and Kimberly had that as part of their profile."

"I'm not sure. I'm not sure how to find out either. All these dating sites have their own jargon and acronyms." Danielle stretched, leaning back into her chair.

Everything had its own jargon and acronyms. "How do people learn what they are? There's got to be some kind of resource. Maybe there'll be something there that can help us."

Danielle's index finger beat out a quick tattoo on the table.

"Internet searches are our friends." She typed *HSIPos acronym list* into the search bar and hit return. "Bingo. There's a forum separate from the app where people give tips, tricks, and explanations."

After a few seconds, she said, "NOO means 'not out in the open.' It lets people know that the person hasn't let their family or friends know about being infected."

Divinia said, "I've been looking at their social media profiles. Look at this," she turned her computer so that Morgan and Danielle could see a series of photographs of all three of their victims. In each one, all three women wore high-necked shirts and blouses that hid the rash on their chests and scarves or chunky necklaces around their necks to hide the lumps that had formed there.

"How hard was it to find those?" Morgan asked.

"Not very. Between having their names and doing a reverse image search, it only took a few minutes." Divinia smoothed her hair back and stretched as well.

"Could that NOO designation be another thing that our guy could be using to choose his victims?" Morgan asked.

Divinia nodded. "Possibly. It would make the women more vulnerable and make it harder to track him. They probably weren't telling anyone about meeting anyone on the site, so they wouldn't be telling their friends or family where or when they were meeting someone."

"Whoa!" Danielle said. "Look at this."

She turned the computer again, so Morgan could read it. There was a post on the forum whose title was "BEWARE IN DC."

Stay away from ManlyMan27! Met this guy at a bar for a drink. After he said he'd walk me back to my car. I thought he was being a gentleman. Turns out he was just trying to get me into a dark place with no witnesses. He punched me in the head! The only thing that saved me was that a security guard came through on a sweep. Guy took off. I've reported him to the app, but his profile is still up.

Spread the word! ManlyMan27 is a total psycho!!!

"Does she say anything about a baseball bat?" Morgan asked. Their unsub had a pretty definite MO.

"Not here, but that doesn't mean he wouldn't have gotten to that if he hadn't been scared off." Danielle turned to Divinia, "Can you help me track down who this woman is? I'd like to talk to her. She might actually be able to give us a description of our murderer."

"What have you got so far?" Divinia asked.

"Here's her profile photo and her username on HSIPos." Danielle hit a few buttons and a ding sounded on Divinia's computer as the files arrived.

"Okay. Give me a minute." Divinia began to work her magic. Her fingers flew so quickly, a dark blur over the keyboard, that Morgan couldn't keep track of what she was doing.

"I've got her socials," Divinia said. "Her name is Gigi Hiller. Give me another five and I'll have her address for you."

Danielle stood. "Come on, Morgan. By the time we get the car out of the garage, Divinia should have the address."

He was already on his feet.

"I'll work on finding the identity of ManlyMan27 while you go," Divinia said.

"Let's go, Morgan. I have a good feeling about this. We may have found our guy."

Morgan held the door open for her and they headed back for the SUV.

CHAPTER TWENTY ONE

Morgan's phone dinged with Gigi Hiller's address before they made it out of the parking garage. Divinia sent a follow-up message letting them know that she'd gone the extra step of making sure the woman was home and would be expecting them.

Morgan plugged the address into the SUV's GPS as Danielle navigated their way out onto the street, and they were off. Danielle took the turn fast enough that everything not secured in the vehicle slid to one side.

"Are we in a hurry?" Morgan asked as he grabbed hold of the bracket handle.

Danielle shrugged. "I'm not sure. My guess is that if we can find that post on the forum, so can the guy who attacked her. If he knows that she can identify him . . ."

"Got it." Plus, they were all aware of the narrow amounts of time between kills. Was the killer escalating? No one wanted to see more bodies pile up. Morgan pulled his seatbelt tighter and sat back to let Danielle concentrate on driving, weaving in and out of traffic on the crowded streets.

Gigi lived in a high-rise apartment building with a doorman. Danielle parked out front and took a look around. "Well, that's a relief. She's probably safe for the moment, at least."

Morgan followed Danielle as she strode up to the doorman and flipped out her badge. "I'm here to see Gigi Hiller."

He was a tall man, but thin. His uniform jacket hung on him. Morgan wasn't sure he offered much security, although he supposed having someone note who went in and out was a deterrent in and of itself. "Ms. Hiller told me to expect you." He opened the door. "She's on floor seven."

"Thanks."

Morgan gave the man a little wave as they walked by and got into the elevator.

Gigi was waiting for them in the hallway outside her apartment when they got off the elevator. She was an attractive young woman, tall and slender with light brown skin and jet-black hair that spilled in curls down to her shoulders. She had on capri-length sweat pants and a tank top. Her feet were bare. "Special Agent Hernandez?" she asked.

Danielle smiled. "That's me," she said, pulling out her badge once again. "Are you okay to talk inside?" She gestured with her head toward the apartment.

"Sure. Why not?"

Morgan glanced over at Danielle. Either Gigi lived alone or she wasn't trying to keep her condition hidden from anyone. She wasn't wearing a scarf and while her top was modest, it wasn't high enough to completely cover the rash on her chest.

He was getting a bad feeling. Gigi didn't seem to be hiding her condition from anyone and her assailant hadn't used a baseball bat. Were there two people out there preying on women with HSI who used the HSIPos dating app?

"Do you want anything? Coffee? Water?" Gigi asked as they went in.

It was a nice apartment. Considerably nicer than the one that Morgan currently rented. Of course, he hadn't expected to still be living in that apartment. He'd thought it was a short-term rental, at best. It had been more than a year now, though. Maybe it was time to upgrade.

"Nothing for us," Danielle said, sitting down on the sofa. Morgan sat next to her. Gigi sat in an overstuffed armchair across from them, picking up a throw pillow and holding it in front of her like a little girl holding a stuffed animal to protect her.

"So what does the FBI want with me?" she asked.

Danielle took out her notebook and flipped it open. "You posted a message on the HSIPos Dating Forum about another one of the app's users attacking you. We were hoping to get more information about what happened."

Gigi threw her hands in the air. "Finally someone's paying attention! I can't get anyone at the app to even email me back." Then she frowned. "But the FBI?"

"There's a possibility what happened to you could be related to another case we're working," Danielle said.

"This guy did this to someone else?" Gigi shook her head, "Bastard."

Morgan liked this woman's fire. Good for her.

"Tell us what happened," Danielle said.

"It's pretty much what I put in that post. I met the guy for a drink. Things were going well, but not that well, you know?" She raised her eyebrows.

94

Danielle nodded. "I know."

Morgan glanced over at her, realizing that he knew next to nothing about Danielle's personal life. Did she date? Did she have a boyfriend? A girlfriend? She didn't wear a ring, so he was fairly certain she wasn't married.

"So he offered to walk me to my car. I'd parked in the garage, but the only space I could get was back in a corner where it was pretty dark. It seemed like a good idea to have some company."

"Smart," Danielle said.

Morgan watched her make a note in her book, admiring the smooth way she encouraged Gigi to keep talking by supporting her — showing she was listening, but not interrupting the flow of the story with questions.

"So anyway, we get to my car and I'm pulling my keys out of my purse. My head was kind of down." She demonstrated how her neck would have been bent as she looked in her purse. "Then I felt something smack me in the back of my head. Hard."

Morgan leaned forward. Could it have been a baseball bat? Could she have been mistaken?

"You're sure he punched you?" Danielle asked. "He didn't have anything with him? A bat or something?"

Gigi paled. "A baseball bat? Like that woman over in the arboretum? It's been on the news all day."

Of course it had. Morgan realized he'd been naive to assume the press wouldn't be all over this. A murder in broad daylight at the National Arboretum? He wondered how long it would take them to connect the other two murders to Sandra Cartmill. Then all hell would probably break loose. They needed to catch this guy, fast, before there was panic throughout the city.

"Not necessarily," Danielle said. "It felt prudent to ask, though."

Gigi sat back again. "Oh. That makes sense, I guess. But no, it was a hard punch with his fist. I know because when I turned, he had his fist cocked to hit me again. Luckily, the security guard in that little motorized car came around the corner just then and I screamed for help. The dude ran."

"Can you describe this man for me?" Danielle asked.

"Tall. White. Reddish blond hair. Blue eyes." She frowned. "Kind of average in most other ways."

"Any scars or tattoos or anything like that?" Danielle asked.

Gigi shook her head. "No. But I've got his license plate number if that'll help."

Morgan thought Danielle was about to fall off the couch. "That would definitely help. If I may ask, how did you manage that?"

"The psycho was parked in the same garage I parked in!" Gigi shook her head as if she had trouble believing it herself. "He went screeching by minutes after the security guard got there. The guard was still making sure I was okay and trying to convince me to go to the hospital to get checked out."

Something was bothering Morgan. "Is there a reason you didn't call the police?"

Gigi looked down at her hands in her lap. "At the time, I was really shaken up. The security guard kept asking me if he could call them, but I just really wanted to go home. Then, once I got home and felt safe, I called and they didn't seem all that interested. They asked if there was any damage to my car, if he'd stolen anything, or if I needed medical attention. When I said no to all that, they practically hung up on me. I figured I missed my window."

Danielle leaned forward. "You haven't. The window is definitely still open. I'd love to have that license plate number."

Picking up her phone, Gigi scrolled for a second and then handed the phone to Danielle. "Here. I took a photo."

Danielle copied the number down and then stood. "Ms. Hiller, thank you so much. You have been a great help. We really appreciate it."

Gigi stood too and walked them to the door. "I just want to be sure that the bastard doesn't do that to anybody else."

"We'll do our best," Danielle assured her.

They rode the elevator down to the lobby. "What do you think?" Morgan asked.

"I think it's an awfully good lead." She looked at him. "A lead we wouldn't have known anything about if you hadn't been able to figure out that they all had the same STI."

Morgan felt a rush of warmth. It felt good to have contributed that way. They stepped out into the lobby and nodded good-bye to the doorman. Once they were back in the car, Danielle pulled out her phone. "Henry, I need you to run a plate for me. I'll text you a photo of it."

She hit a few buttons and then sat back. It was only a matter of seconds before Henry replied. "The car is registered to an Aidan Sherrer. I'll text you his address."

"Great work." Danielle put the address into her GPS.

Morgan looked at the map and frowned. He'd expected the address to be in the Trinidad neighborhood. This one wasn't. It was over in Columbia Heights, far from the triangle that Henry's map had sketched.

"Let's go pay Mr. Sherrer a visit," Danielle said.

CHAPTER TWENTY TWO

Morgan flipped the car's passenger side visor down. The sun was getting low in the sky and the angle made him squint. He could practically see the steam rising off the roadway as the heat rose again. Danielle stared straight ahead, eyes protected with sunglasses, jaw resolute.

She switched lanes, passing a car on the right, then slipping back in front of it smoothly.

"I take it we're still in a hurry," Morgan said.

"I'm not sure. I don't feel like taking any chances, though. If this is our guy, he's killed at least three times and made one other attempt. There's nothing holding him back anymore." She exited the Beltway, leaving behind the green lushness of the surrounding area and plunged back into the heart of DC. "There are no more lines for him to cross."

The house they pulled up in front of was two stories with peeling paint that might have been yellow at some point but had faded to a dingy gray. The yard, such as it was, was mainly taken over by weeds. It was a far cry from Gigi Hiller's sleek Adams Morgan high-rise. Angelica and Kimberly had both been employed in good jobs with no dependents. Could part of Sherrer's motivation have to do with women who were more successful than him? That ManlyMan moniker he'd chosen for himself spoke of some deep-seated insecurity. Could a sense of impotence have been spurring him on to more and more violence?

They got out of the car. Danielle put her suit jacket back on. "Stay behind me as we go up, okay?"

Morgan nodded.

"I mean it, Morgan. We don't know what this guy is capable of. I want you with me. Your observations on this case have been too valuable to make you wait in the car, but I also want you safe." She tugged her jacket straight. Grabbing her phone, she called into the office. "Hi, Henry. Morgan and I are at Sherrer's home."

Before she could say more, a crashing sound rang out from the house followed quickly by a scream.

"Something's going on inside the house. Morgan and I are going in. Send backup. NOW!" She dropped the phone in her pocket and took off running toward the house.

Morgan was right on her heels, glad those morning runs were starting to pay off.

A woman's voice was pleading. "Please, Aidan! I'm sorry!"

"Aidan Sherrer!" Danielle yelled out from the front porch, weapon drawn, holding it in both hands, but pointed down toward the ground. "FBI! Open up!"

"Help!" the woman yelled. "He's gonna kill me. I really think he's gonna kill me this time."

Morgan's gut clenched at the "this time." Whoever this woman was, she didn't deserve to live like that.

"I'm coming in, Sherrer!" Danielle yelled. She motioned to Morgan to try the door.

The knob turned smoothly in his hand and he pushed the door open, careful to keep it from banging back at them from the wall.

"Shut up, bitch!" a man yelled. A woman whimpered in reply.

Danielle tapped her chest and pointed in the direction of the noise. Then she pointed at Morgan and motioned him to the side. He nodded and flattened himself against the wall.

"Sherrer, this is Special Agent Danielle Hernandez. I'm coming in. Drop whatever weapons you might have." In three decisive strides, Danielle was down the hall and making the turn into the kitchen. "Drop the knife, Sherrer!"

Morgan sidled up to the doorway and looked in. Danielle had her gun pointed at a man standing in the middle of the kitchen. He held a knife. He was a big guy. Beefy. White with reddish hair. A woman lay at his feet, curled into a ball, trying to protect her face and head.

"I said to drop the knife!" Danielle barked. "Now!"

Sherrer's eyes darted between the woman on the floor and Danielle. "This isn't any of your business. Get out of here."

"Drop the knife and we'll talk about what my business is here," Danielle said, her gun never wavering.

Morgan slipped the rest of the way into the room. Danielle nodded her head slightly to the right and Morgan moved in that direction, realizing that Sherrer now had to divide his attention between the two of them. Morgan took a few more steps to the right.

Morgan took a deep breath and said, "Hey, man. We really just want to talk. Why don't you put the knife down? We can make sure your lady friend here is okay and then discuss this."

Sherrer's attention shifted to Morgan and Danielle slid ever so slightly to her left, further widening the space between them that

Sherrer would have to cover.

"Who the hell are you?" The knife shook in Sherrer's hand. Whether it was fear or adrenaline was anyone's guess.

"My name's Dr. Morgan Stark. I'm a doc over at Georgetown Hospital." It was a small lie, but he doubted anyone would care. "I'd love to check out this lady, make sure she's okay."

"Please, Aidan." The woman's voice was nearly a whisper.

Sherrer spit on the floor next to the woman. "I told you to be quiet. I have to think."

Morgan crouched down on the floor so he could better see the woman's face. "I'm Morgan. What's your name?"

"Virginia. Virginia Sherrer." She was pretty. Or probably was when her face wasn't tear-streaked and one of her eyes wasn't swelling shut. A trickle of blood dripped from her upper lip.

"Great. That's great." Morgan looked up at Sherrer. "How about you let Virginia come with me, Aidan. I can look after her, make sure she's okay."

Sherrer shifted to be between Morgan and Virginia. Over Sherrer's shoulder, Morgan saw Danielle give him a little nod. Keep going. Keep distracting him.

"She's not going anywhere," Sherrer said.

Morgan stood and took a step back, hands held up in front of him. "Okay. We can stay here. That eye doesn't look great. How about you let me get some ice on it for her?"

Sherrer took another step toward him, letting his knife hand drop a little lower. "Get lost. We don't need you interfering here."

Danielle soundlessly slid her gun back into its holster and while Sherrer was still focused on Morgan, she stepped forward grabbing the arm that held the knife and twisting it up behind him.

Sherrer must have heard her at the last second. While she still had a hold of the arm with the knife, he swung at her head with his left hand.

Danielle ducked but not quite fast enough. Sherrer's fist connected with the side of her head. For a second, she looked dazed. Sherrer raised his hand to punch her again. If he connected, Morgan wasn't sure Danielle would be able to hold onto that knife hand. If Sherrer got free, Morgan wasn't sure what he would do. Visions of the kind of damage a knife that big could do flashed through his brain. He'd stitched up more than a few, but he knew that sometimes no amount of stitching would help.

He sprang forward, kicking out with his right leg aiming for the peroneal nerve, just above Sherer's knee. The man screamed and crumpled to the ground. In seconds, Danielle had Sherrer's knife hand pinned under the heel of her shoe. The hand opened releasing the knife and Morgan kicked it away into the corner. He heard sirens approaching and hoped like hell they were on their way here.

"I think you broke my fucking leg!" Sherrer yelled.

"Not likely. Just clipped you in the right spot." Morgan knelt down next to Virginia. "Probably feels a little numb right now, but you'll bounce right back."

Danielle drew her gun and pointed it at Sherrer. "Roll onto your stomach and put your hands behind your head." Her chest heaved, but her grip on the gun was steady, unwavering.

Morgan helped Virginia sit up. "Okay. Let's get you checked over."

Her pulse was fast, but steady. No bones seemed to be broken. He sat back on his heels. "Can you tell me what hurts?"

"My eye," she said.

"Yeah, you're going to have quite a shiner, but nothing's broken, which is good." He stood up and opened the freezer. Finding a bag of peas, he handed them to Virginia and gestured for her to hold it against her eye.

The front door banged open. "FBI!"

"We're back here, Henry," Danielle called, her gun still trained on the back of Sherrer's head.

Henry came around the corner, his eyes widening at the scene in front of him.

"Cuff him, please," Danielle said. Only when Sherrer was cuffed did she holster her weapon. A vein in her throat pulsed in a quick rhythm. She inhaled slowly and exhaled even more slowly. Morgan could see her visibly getting her nerves back under control.

Virginia huddled closer to Morgan. "What's going to happen now?"

"First, I think we need to get you checked out more thoroughly." He looked over at Henry, "Is there an ambulance coming? Paramedics?"

"Should be here in a couple of minutes," he said. "I wanted to make sure the scene was secured first."

Danielle nodded her approval. "Good thinking."

Outside, Morgan heard more vehicles arriving and doors slamming. Henry went out to usher people in. Morgan stepped back as the paramedics went immediately to Virginia. Two other agents that Morgan recognized from the bullpen on the fifth floor came in and helped Sherrer to his feet. The man's eyes blazed with hatred. "You better keep your mouth shut, Virginia!" he spat out.

Danielle moved around in front of him. "Or what? Are you threatening her?"

Sherrer looked like he might be about to lunge forward at Danielle, but thought better of it and looked down at his shoes.

"I thought not." She turned to the two agents holding him. "Take him to Interview Room Three. I'll be there soon."

They nodded and escorted Sherrer out of the room. By then the paramedics had Virginia on a gurney. In minutes, the room that had been bustling was empty.

Danielle pulled out her phone. "Hi, Divinia. Get a search warrant for Sherrer's residence, please. I want to find the man's damn baseball bat. It's got to be here somewhere."

She hung up.

"Couldn't we search right now?" Morgan asked.

Danielle looked around, hands on hips. "If it was sitting out in plain sight, we might be okay, but I don't want to take a chance on it being inadmissible in court. We had exigent circumstances to enter the home. I don't want to push it." She rubbed her hands together. "Now let's go hear what Mr. Sherrer has to say for himself."

CHAPTER TWENTY THREE

Morgan watched the day fade to twilight as they returned to headquarters. He let his head loll back against the headrest and listened in as Danielle placed a call.

"Sheehan here," a male voice said, sounding weary.

"Hey, Brett. It's Danielle Hernandez. I think we might have our guy." Morgan could hear the tempered excitement in her voice.

"The baseball bat guy?" Sheehan said, interest clearly piqued.

"Yeah. Although he had a knife this time. We're in the process of getting a warrant to search the house and his vehicle to see if we can find anything. We'll also check into phone records, see if his phone pings anywhere near the crime scenes in the right time frame."

Morgan made mental notes on the way Danielle processed each scene. She was methodical, but not completely inflexible.

"Excellent!" Sheehan said.

Danielle smiled at the man's enthusiasm. "I'm on my way back to headquarters to interview him. Want to observe?"

"You bet I do."

Morgan broke in, "You also might want to send someone to the hospital to interview his wife. She's the one he was about to cut when we showed up. Name's Virginia Sherrer. Or close enough."

"He's one of those then?" Sheehan sounded disgusted.

Danielle sighed, "Appears to be."

"Great. I've got someone who specializes in domestic abuse. She's got a great track record of helping these women get out of those situations. I'll send her to the hospital to talk to Ms. Sherrer. I'll be at headquarters in about thirty minutes."

"Sounds perfect."

Danielle hung up.

"You trust him?" Morgan asked, not sure about the relationship between the different law enforcement entities.

"He's a good guy." Danielle yawned. "He might be able to hold Sherrer on the assault charges more easily than we can on the possible serial angle. It'll give us a chance to gather more evidence and get his wife some place safe."

They entered the building and made their way up to the fifth floor. The bullpen area was empty, but Morgan could hear people in the conference room. The smell of pizza hit Morgan's nose before they rounded the corner. His stomach growled. When was the last time he'd eaten?

"Help yourself to a slice," Henry said, turning at the sound of them entering.

He grabbed a slice of pizza and devoured it, then wiped his hands on a napkin. Danielle also grabbed a slice. Neither of them sat. He was chomping at the bit to hear what Sherrer would have to say for himself, especially under Danielle's adroit questioning.

He also wanted to get a better look at him to see if he had any symptoms of HSI.

The security guard from downstairs buzzed them. "I've got a Detective Sheehan here to see you, Special Agent Hernandez."

"Great. I'll be right down." Danielle stood up and brushed off her hands. "I'll go get Sheehan and then we'll get to work on Sherrer."

"Who do I owe for the pizza?" Morgan asked Henry and Divinia after Danielle left.

Henry held up his hand. "No worries. With all you've been doing for us on this case, a few slices are the least we can do."

"Thanks."

Danielle returned to the conference room with Sheehan. "Ready, Morgan?"

He nodded and the three made their way down the hall.

"I think Morgan and I should be the ones to go in first," Danielle told Sheehan. "We can hold you as backup in case we can't get what we need from him."

"Sure. Happy to watch the vaunted FBI interview techniques in action," Sheehan grinned at her.

Morgan looked back and forth between them. There seemed to be an extra charge in the air. Was their relationship more than professional?

He followed Danielle as they left Sheehan in the observation room and went into the interview room where Sherrer waited. They sat down across from him and Danielle folded her hands on the table top. "So, Mr. Sherrer, how about you tell us about what we walked in on at your house this afternoon."

Her tone was calm and respectful. Morgan noted how open-ended she'd left the question. Was she giving Sherrer enough rope to hang himself with?

104

"You misinterpreted what you saw. Ginny fell. The linoleum in that old kitchen is in terrible shape. She tripped on a spot where it was torn." Sherrer's voice was without heat, as if he was just a guy explaining a miscommunication.

Morgan felt steam building up between his ears. Did this abuser really expect them to accept this kind of bullshit? He must not have been hiding how he felt because Danielle put a hand on his leg under the table for a moment, as if asking him to wait.

He took a deep breath and counted as he blew it out. He'd wait, but he didn't think there was any way he could pretend to be the good cop with this dirtbag. He took a moment to examine what he could of Mr. Sherrer's condition. There was no visible rash on his chest, no lump on his neck, and his fingernails were healthy and pink-looking. The man definitely didn't have HSI.

"And you were holding a knife, why?" Danielle's tone also stayed conversational, as if they were talking about the weather.

"I was getting ready to make dinner. Seriously, this is all a misunderstanding. I'm sure Ginny will clear it up. Let me talk to her and we'll all probably have a good laugh about it later," Sherrer smiled at Danielle, ignoring Morgan.

Morgan definitely wasn't going to be laughing. He had a pretty good idea of what kind of conversation Aidan would have with Virginia if they let him. It would be some combination of threats and gaslighting.

Shuffling through some of the papers in front of her, Danielle said, "You mean like you did the other three times that the police have been called to your residence?" The substance of the question was accusatory, but still her tone wasn't.

Sherrer's jaw clenched for a second. "Nosy neighbors. Always getting into our business. You'll see that Ginny never pressed charges." He was doing his best to sound nonchalant, but a trickle of sweat ran down the side of his face and he kept licking his lips, as if his mouth had suddenly gone dry.

"I do see that." Danielle tapped the papers back into a neat pile and set them down. Then she folded her hands on top of them. "While whatever you were doing to your wife might well get you locked up, that isn't actually what we're here to talk to you about, however."

Sherrer's eyes widened. "It's not?"

"Nope." She smiled, then pulled crime scene photos out and laid them in front of Sherrer, one by one. "We want to talk to you about Kimberly Samson, Angelica McNally, and Sandra Cartmill." She tapped a photo of each woman's ruined face and body as she said each name.

Sherrer pushed back from the table as if he needed distance from the photos. "What? No! I don't know who those people are. I definitely didn't do anything like that!" He tugged at the handcuffs that kept him clipped to the metal rod embedded in the table.

Morgan watched him carefully. Was that instant revulsion an act? Was trying to pull away from the table a calculated move? Or was Sherrer honestly shocked and revolted?

"You sure about that, Mr. Sherrer? We're pulling your cell phone records now and we'll be searching your house soon. Are you positive we won't find any communications between you and these women? How about baseball bats? Are we going to find any of those in your house?" Danielle's eyes gleamed.

"Baseball bats? Why . . . Oh, that's what did that?" Sherrer nodded toward the photos.

Danielle leaned in. "You tell us. What exactly did you use to kill these women? And why?"

"I didn't kill anybody! Stop saying that!" He tugged at the chain harder.

"We've already found your profile on HSIPos. We'll be connecting this all up soon. You might as well tell us now." Danielle sat back in her chair, looking relaxed. "Save everyone some time and aggravation. It might make people more inclined to cut you a break. It's in your best interest to confess."

"HSIPos? All these chicks were on HSIPos?" Sherrer sounded confused, but not about what HSIPos was.

"Mmhmm. Just like you were. That's how you found them, right?" Danielle asked.

Sherrer shook his head back and forth. "No. I mean, yes. I was using the app, but not to do something like that."

"Really? Because it seems like you used it to find Gigi Hiller and then tried to beat her up in a dark parking garage," Danielle said.

Sherrer looked around the room as if there might be some way to escape. There wasn't, of course. "Gigi? You spoke to Gigi?" He dropped his head. "I should have realized she was different and left her alone."

"Different how?" Danielle kept her voice even, but Morgan saw the way her fingers tightened around her pen. She knew she was getting somewhere.

"She wasn't ashamed. All the other women I met on there and on

106

the other apps for people with STIs were so embarrassed, like they thought they were the only people in the world who had sex." He looked over at Morgan as if he might get some kind of agreement.

The last thing Morgan wanted was to feel any connection with this creep, but if it would help put him away, he'd do it. He'd control his temper. He leaned forward. "So that's what drew you to them? How ashamed they were?" He framed it as if it was the women's fault they were embarrassed by their condition and that that had been what attracted Sherrer to them.

"Yeah. Totally. See, I knew they wouldn't tell anybody what happened. If they did, they'd have to explain how they met me and that would mean they would have to tell everybody they had HSI." Sherrer sat up straighter, less worried now. "They were so clearly embarrassed. I knew they wouldn't say anything, but Gigi . . . well, she didn't try to cover that rash."

Morgan hoped that would make him more forthcoming. He himself would be taking a shower after talking to this guy.

Danielle pushed the photos forward. "No one was going to be talking to anyone after you did this to them."

"That's what I'm saying. I didn't do that to anyone! I'd get them somewhere quiet and private and knock them around a bit and then take whatever jewelry or money they had on them. They'd been begging to give it to me to get me to leave them alone." Sherrer made it sound like it was the most reasonable thing to have done.

"What happened with Kimberly, Angelica, and Sandra then? Did they not agree to give you anything? Or did they not have enough?" Danielle asked.

Something wasn't adding up for Morgan here. Kimberly and Angelica had still had cash and credit cards in their wallets. Nothing of value was taken from Kimberly's home. If Sherrer's whole motivation was to rob them, why had he left such easy pickings on the ground?

"No! That's what I'm telling you. I had nothing to do with those women. I didn't kill anyone. I maybe roughed a few of them up, but nothing big. Nothing like that." He gestured to the photos with his chin.

Danielle picked up her folders, but left the photos on the table in front of Sherrer and headed to the door. Before she left, she turned and said, "We'll see about that. We're collecting evidence now. You might want to get ahead of this. Tell me what happened. Maybe I can get the charges on your lessened."

"There's nothing to tell. You're not gonna find anything that links me to those women because I didn't do that."

"Sure you didn't." Danielle and Morgan walked out, letting the door to the interview room bang shut behind them.

"He's all yours for now," Danielle said to Sheehan. "I'll be in touch when we get the evidence we need to tie him to the murders."

Sheehan shook his head. "What a piece of work. I'll take him downtown and get him processed. I'll let you know if he lets anything else slip."

"Thanks." Danielle leaned back against the wall and closed her eyes. The shadows under her eyes stood out in stark relief.

Morgan looked at his watch. It was after nine o'clock. They'd started the day at eight in the morning. Twelve-hour days and more were par for the course for a physician, especially one who worked in a hospital. It still took its toll, though.

"What was that you were telling me about burnout?" he asked.

She smiled without opening her eyes. "I was telling you that getting rest when you can is important and I think we've earned a good night's sleep." She opened her eyes. "I think we've got our guy. It's all a matter of collecting evidence now. Let's get some rest and hit it hard tomorrow."

Morgan didn't feel quite as confident that they had their killer. There were too many things that didn't feel quite right. The rage against women was there. The guy was on HSIPos and admitted to using it to lure victims. But if his motive was robbery, why didn't he take the women's wallets? Or electronics from Kimberly Samson's home? Then there was the knife. That wasn't the unsub's preferred means of aggression. Plus, it was clear how much of a mess attacking with a baseball bat made. Yet, there hadn't been a drop of blood visible anywhere on Sherrer. He could have had time to shower and clean up, but what about his clothes? Maybe they'd find them when they searched the house. Morgan shook his head. He'd feel more certain once they found the baseball bat or the burner phone Sherrer had used to connect with the victims.

Meanwhile, Danielle was right. It was time to get some rest. They'd learn more tomorrow.

CHAPTER TWENTY FOUR

The man paced back and forth in the small park. It was only a little spot of green in the middle of the block, but she had said it was what had made her rent the apartment. They'd even brought a picnic lunch here once. She'd laughed and said it was silly, but he could tell it had pleased her.

He wondered if any of the dirtbags she was meeting on that app did things like take her on picnics. He doubted it.

From where he stood, he could see her apartment. The windows were dark, so he couldn't see in. Locked up tight as a drum too. He'd checked all the doors and windows he could get to, including the one to the fire escape, and each one was secured. Where the hell was she? It was after ten o'clock and she still wasn't home.

She was probably with some other guy. Some guy that she wanted more than she wanted him. So much for that whole "it wasn't him, it was her" line. Her stupid excuses meant nothing. She'd said she didn't want to be with him anymore because she'd gotten that stupid STI and didn't want to give it to him. She clearly wasn't sitting home alone, though. She was just like all those other women on the app. They all needed to be punished. They were all liars and cheaters.

Except she wasn't like the rest of them. He stopped pacing and sat down on a concrete bench. She wasn't like anyone else. She'd been special. He'd tried to let her know that with everything that he said and did. With impromptu picnics and little gifts.

It hadn't helped. She'd still dumped him.

She'd walked away, washing her hands of him as if he was the one with the dirty virus.

It wasn't fair!

Well, he would show her how unfair something could be. Just like he'd shown those other three whores.

At the thought of them, the pressure began to build inside him again. It was like there were bees buzzing in his head, making it hard to think clearly. All he wanted was the sweet release he'd felt every time he'd swung that baseball bat and felt its satisfying thunk against human flesh and bone.

He wanted it again, even though he'd barely showered off the last of the Sandra Cartmill's blood. Had that been only earlier today? It seemed like so long ago. It seemed like years.

At that thought, he sagged a bit. He'd had a busy day and he was tired. He'd come back tomorrow. She'd be home eventually, and if she wasn't, he could go back on the app to see if there were any more women volunteering to be his next victim. He headed for his car, tapping the ground gently with his baseball bat as he went.

CHAPTER TWENTY FIVE

Outside on the sidewalk in front of the FBI building, Morgan called a ride share. He'd told Danielle he didn't need a ride home, that she should get herself to her own place and get some rest. He programmed in St. Mary's Hospital's address into the app instead of his apartment, though. That was where they'd taken Virginia Sherrer.

The silver Honda that the app had told him was arriving soon pulled up to the curb and he got in. "Hi."

"Hey, man," the thirty-something hipster said from the front seat. "Help yourself to some water."

Grateful, Morgan pulled one of the water bottles out of a small ice chest on the floor and slugged it down. "Thanks. I didn't realize how thirsty I was."

"Hydrate and thrive, man." The driver paused. "Everything okay? Kind of late to be going to the hospital."

"Just checking on someone there."

"Oh, well, I guess that's all right then." He pulled up in front of the hospital's main entrance.

"Thanks for the ride and the water," Morgan said as he got out, hitting the button to give the guy five stars and a good tip.

The man leaned out of the window. "Peace out. Hope your friend is okay." Then he was gone.

Morgan stepped up to the doors and they whooshed open in front of him.

The fluorescent lights inside the hospital were bright and the slight buzz from them made his head throb. He took a deep breath, inhaling that faint antiseptic smell that underlay everything at the hospital. He supposed it was a little like his version of Proust's Madeleine. For so many years, this had been where he felt he truly belonged. Would he ever find that again? Shaking his head at his own maudlin thoughts, he made his way to the emergency room. He walked up to the desk and showed the nurse his credentials. "I was hoping to see Virginia Sherrer."

The nurse looked up at him and then tapped a few keys on her computer. "She's in bay six. You can go on in." She hit a button under

111

the desk and the doors into the treatment area swung open. The place was busy. It was a Friday night after all and late enough that people would have already been at the bars for a while. At least it wasn't a full moon.

Morgan dodged around an orderly pushing a wheelchair towards a bay. No one looked twice at him. They were all too busy with their own work to wonder what he was doing there.

He found Virginia in bay six sitting up on a gurney, feet dangling over the edge like a little girl. She jumped as Morgan came through the curtains around the bed, and he cursed himself for not going a little slower. Of course, she'd be jumpy. For all she knew, it could have been Aidan coming in to harass her. He held his hands up in front of him, palms facing her, and tried to give her a reassuring smile. "Hi, Virginia. Remember me? We, uh, met at your house earlier."

She nodded. The eye that wasn't swollen shut filled with tears. "I remember. I don't remember your name, though."

"Morgan Stark." He stuck out his hand and she shook it gingerly.

"I already told everything to that police lady," Virginia said. "I don't know what else I can tell you."

"Oh, I didn't come here to ask questions." Why did he come here? He wasn't sure of the exact source of the impulse, but he knew he wouldn't have been able to sleep without checking in to see how she was. He'd been like that with patients at the hospital too. He couldn't quite go home and go to sleep without one last round of checking in on everyone at the end of the day. "I wanted to see if you needed anything."

She looked down at her hands and then back up at him. "Honestly? I'm really hungry. I haven't had anything since lunch and they told me I can't leave here yet. The police lady went to make arrangements for a place for me to stay, but I don't know where she is or when she'll be back."

Damn. He should have thought of that. "How about I go find a vending machine or something? I could get you a bag of chips and a candy bar or something like that."

Her eyes went wide. "Oh, no. Aidan doesn't allow me to have junk food like that. He says it'll make me fat."

Morgan took a second before he spoke, trying to calm the anger that had flared up in him. "Aidan's not here and you need some calories. Your body burns a lot when it's trying to heal. It won't make you fat. I'll be right back."

He returned to the nurses' station. "I'm looking for some food for

112

the patient in bed six."

The nurse looked up and then over at the board and nodded. "She's clear for food. The only thing we have here is some Jell-O. The cafeteria is closed, but there are some vending machines down the hall." She pointed the way.

"Thanks." Morgan walked in the direction she'd indicated and found the machines. After some deliberation, he came away with some peanut butter crackers and fruit snacks. As he approached Virginia's bed again, he heard the murmur of female voices from behind the curtain. Possibly one of the doctors had come back to do another check or maybe the police officer had returned. He didn't want to startle Virginia again or invade her privacy so he cleared his throat and said, "Virginia, it's Morgan. I've got some food for you. Okay if I come in?"

The curtain snatched back, and he found himself face-to-face with Danielle. In unison, they both said, "What are you doing here?"

Then Danielle shook her head and stepped aside so he could come in. He set his finds down on the bed in front of Virginia. "These were the healthiest snacks I could find."

"Oh, these are great." She ripped open the package and nibbled her way through a peanut butter cracker.

Morgan turned to Danielle. "I just wanted to make sure she was okay."

She nodded. "Me too."

They might come at problems from completely different directions, but in the end, they were both there for the same reason. To help people. To protect them. He'd come to appreciate Danielle's intelligence and her strength. Now he'd gotten a little sense of her kindness as well. Were all FBI agents like this? He doubted it.

"Where's Aidan?" Virginia asked.

Danielle sat down in a chair next to the bed. "He's being processed down at Police Headquarters."

Virginia looked back and forth between them. "But you two aren't police. You yelled something about the FBI when you came in. Why's the FBI interested in Aidan?"

Danielle crossed her legs. For a moment, Morgan wasn't sure if she was going to answer or not. Then she said, "We suspect your husband has been using a dating app to target certain women."

"Target them for what?" Virginia asked, brow furrowed.

"We're still figuring that out. He said it was to rob them." Danielle cocked her head to one side, clearly watching for Virginia's reaction.

Morgan held his breath, waiting to hear what Virginia might say.

Had she known what her husband was doing? Or had she been oblivious? He was clearly controlling and abusive. He'd probably talked circles around her so many times that she didn't know what to believe.

Virginia went very still for a moment and then sighed. She unhooked a bracelet she was wearing and handed it to Danielle. "I knew there was something not right when he gave me this. I could tell that it wasn't new."

Morgan reached into one of the drawers of the chest of cabinets against the wall and pulled out a small plastic bag that would normally be used to hold samples. Danielle dropped the bracelet in, he sealed it and handed it back to her. Who knew if there'd be any forensic evidence on it, but it was better not to take a chance.

"How long ago did he give it to you?" Danielle asked.

Morgan frowned. There'd been no mention of missing jewelry in any of the cases. Were there other victims they didn't know about?

Virginia kicked her feet against the side of the bed. "I'm not exactly sure, but I think it was right after Valentine's Day. He said it was a belated present."

Valentine's Day had been months ago. As far as Morgan knew — which meant as far as the FBI knew — the first victim was killed earlier this week.

"Has he brought home anything else that you were suspicious about?" Danielle asked.

"He's been more flush than usual, lately. That's for sure. Seems like he's got cash on him all the time." Virginia ate a fruit snack, chewing it thoughtfully. "That's all I've seen that I can remember."

But there'd been cash in all three victims' wallets, not to mention credit cards. Something wasn't right here.

"Well, that's plenty. We really appreciate it." Danielle stood up. "You should probably get some rest. Thanks for your time, Virginia. Good luck."

"Thanks for the snacks! Good night." Virginia waved at them as they left.

Morgan shook his head. She seemed so calm for someone in her situation. Maybe it was shock. Or maybe she was just used to this level of drama in her life. He couldn't imagine living like that.

"Come on, Morgan," Danielle said. "I'll give you a ride home. Make sure you actually go home this time."

"What about you?" Morgan snorted. "You didn't take your own advice either, now did you? Are you the kettle or the pot?"

114

"Neither. I'm going home now. I swear. I'm beat. I just wasn't sure I'd sleep without knowing that she was being taken care of." Her usual stride had slowed considerably. She was definitely dragging.

Morgan pushed open the doors that led to the outside, and they stepped out into the night. The air was still muggy, but without the sun beating down on them, it had a soft feel, almost like a caress.

Morgan understood the urge to check on Virginia. "She seems like a sweet lady. How does someone like that get hooked up with a piece of work like Sherrer?"

Danielle shook her head. "The world is full of mysteries."

"Any word on anything from the search of his house and car?" Morgan asked.

"Nope." Danielle blew out a breath as she led the way to the SUV. "Nothing significant yet."

Morgan glanced at his watch. It had been hours now. Surely they would have found the bat and the clothes by now if they were there. He was no fan of Aidan Sherrer, but he also wasn't sure the man was their murderer.

CHAPTER TWENTY SIX

Morgan said good-bye to Danielle outside his apartment building and made his way up to his place. The first thing he did was strip off the clothes he'd been wearing and get in the shower. The hot water cascaded over him, washing away the physical sweat and grime of the day, but not the emotional grind.

It was hard to get the mental image of banged up Virginia Sherrer sitting quietly in her hospital bed, grateful for peanut butter crackers, out of his head. How did she end up with a guy like Sherrer? How did any of those women that he'd apparently terrorized and robbed end up with him at all?

He toweled off and padded over to his computer. Maybe there'd be hints that could help him answer those questions on the HSIPos website. He could look at Sherrer's profile and see how he presented himself. What had been the name he'd gone under? ManlyMan27?

Morgan logged on, but couldn't get far without creating a profile. The last thing he wanted was to have his name and photo on a dating app for people with STIs. He could just imagine how that would play with the doctors who would decide his fate in a few months.

So, a fake profile was the answer. His fingers froze over the keyboard. A fake profile. One that might interest their unsub if he was still out there.

First, he looked at the profiles of the murdered women. They'd already attracted the unsub. Maybe he'd find a common thread that would guide him in making his own fake profile. No one had taken their profiles down yet. Most likely, their families didn't even know that the profiles existed. Their friends might not either. The women had kept their health issues very quiet, mortified by their status as people with active STIs.

He shook his head. It was one of the issues with getting people treatment. So much shame and self-reproach clouded people's judgment.

Morgan looked over their profiles, copying down phrases, abbreviations, and acronyms to use and then went to work. His goal was to create something that would draw the killer's interest if he was still out there.

All three women were light-haired and white, so he searched through stock photos until he found a photo of a woman who looked like the other three and whose neck was covered with a scarf. He needed to make sure the killer would understand that this woman was still hiding her symptoms from the world, even in a place where everyone else shared the same issues.

He put it all together, named his fake profile Ivy, hit publish, and then pushed back from the desk. It was nearly 2 a.m. Time to get some sleep.

CHAPTER TWENTY SEVEN

The next morning dawned hot and muggy, but Morgan still went through his new morning routine. Despite feeling a little bleary, he hit the sidewalk and went on his three-mile route. Even though he got an early start, it was nearly eighty degrees already and humid. He arrived back home breathing hard and dripping with sweat but feeling better than he had all those mornings after he'd lulled himself to sleep with a combination of scotch and self-pity.

He ran up the stairs, not wanting to subject anyone else who might be in the elevator to how he might smell. He hit the button to start the coffee maker and by the time he was out of the shower, his caffeine hit was hot and waiting for him.

It was only then that he allowed himself to take a look at HSIPos.

He was sorely disappointed. No messages.

Frowning, he poured himself another cup of coffee and then compared his fake profile with the ones for the murdered women. What was he missing?

While he'd deliberately chosen a stock photo of a woman wearing a shirt with a high neckline and a scarf around her neck, he hadn't really emphasized a need for secrecy in the bio that he'd written. He rubbed at his chin as he looked at the words used in the other bios. He added a sentence about the need for discretion and stressing privacy, and he added interests and hobbies that were all relatively solitary.

He made himself eggs and toast and texted Danielle.

Anything?

She texted back: *Patience, grasshopper. Nothing yet.*

Morgan: *Anything I can do?*

Danielle: *Sit tight. I'll be in touch, but I think we're wrapping this one up.*

Morgan sighed. He hoped she was right, but he still had his doubts. As if in answer, his phone buzzed with a notification from HSIPos. He went back to his computer and brought up his profile.

Ivy had gotten two messages!

Hey, pretty lady! Love your profile. I'm also in DC and love hiking and cooking. Maybe we could cook something up together?

118

Morgan shook his head. Seriously? Was this the kind of lame innuendo that women had to deal with on dating sites?

The next message confirmed that.

Hey, hot stuff! You can fry up my sausage any time.

Morgan deleted both messages and sat back, frustrated. Those two guys were creepy, but possibly too creepy. He couldn't imagine any woman wanting to meet up with them and whoever the killer was knew how to make the women feel safe enough to engage with him. He looked at the other women's profiles again and added in the NOO — Not Out in the Open — designation to his fake profile.

He cleaned up his breakfast dishes and looked around the apartment, unsure of what to do next.

Once again, he sank down into a chair and wondered what the hell he was going to do with himself for his six months of suspension from the hospital.

He had no hobbies. There'd never been time. No, that wasn't quite true. He'd never made the time. Every review he'd ever had, every reference from a professor, every comment from a patient had always said the same things. Morgan was focused, driven, and intent. That had seemed like a good thing.

Sadly, that good thing seemed to have a flip side.

Without something to focus on, he felt aimless. How was he going to fill his time?

He could train for a marathon, but you could only run so many hours a day. He could take up hiking or woodworking or — what had Angelica McNally told her father she was studying at the community college? Underwater basket weaving?

None of it appealed to him.

He was a problem solver. That had been what had really been behind most of his career: figuring out difficult diagnoses, finding answers when everyone else had been asking the wrong questions, and fashioning solutions that improved the lives of patients.

Working with Danielle felt like a continuation of that: investigating cases, finding the connections that revealed answers, and bringing answers to grieving families about what had happened to their loved ones.

He wished someone had been able to do that for him and his family after his sister disappeared. He'd been too young and too close to it all to be able to do that then. It would have been good to have someone like Danielle on the case.

His phone buzzed with a notification from HSIPos. Probably

another creep, but he had to check. He went back to the computer to find a message from someone calling himself Scott Elias.

Hi, Ivy. Nice to "meet" you. I also enjoy cooking at home and going hiking. Have you spent much time in the Blue Ridge Mountains? The Luray Caves are amazing. What are your favorite cuisines to cook?

Morgan went to Scott's profile. The guy looked normal. Morgan didn't have any other word for it. White guy. Average height and weight. No visible scars or tattoos. Why was that ringing a bell? Oh, yeah. That was how Cory Smithson had described Angelica McNally. He'd said she seemed normal. Maybe normal was the thing that made all these women feel safe enough to meet this guy.

Morgan did a quick internet search on Blue Ridge Mountain hikes and another on cooking trends and then sent a reply.

Hi, Scott! Nice to "meet" you too. I've never been to Luray. Had a great time at White Rock Falls, though. So beautiful and serene. I've been focusing more on ingredients than types of cuisines. Very into cooking with locally grown foods. Plus, who doesn't love a farmers' market? You?

He got an immediate response.

Haha. Absolutely on the farmers' markets. Have you been to Mount Vernon Triangle? Never been to White Rock Falls. You've definitely peaked my interest, though. I'd love to see them. Any chance you'd be available for a hike today?

Morgan stared at the response for a moment. Today? That was moving pretty quickly. It had been a long time since Morgan had been on the dating scene, but he was reasonably certain that that kind of over-eagerness was frowned upon. Something there bothered him too. He just wasn't quite sure what.

Probably not today. What about next week some time?

Unfortunately, I'm going out of town on business next week and the next few days are going to be taken up with preparing for that trip. It's really today or not for a few weeks.

Every hair on Morgan's neck went up. What the hell? Who pressures a woman that way?

A killer. That's who. Hadn't the killer pressured Angelica into meeting him quickly too?

And then it hit him. The other thing that bothered him about the messages. This man claimed to have his interest peaked rather than piqued. The killer had made the same error when he'd messaged Angelica.

Aidan Sherrer might be an abusive son of a bitch, but he wasn't their killer. Whoever Morgan was messaging with right now was. He was sure of it.

But the killer was still only a profile on the dating app, just as Morgan was. He could be anyone. Morgan needed something more, something the FBI could track.

Okay. I might be able to go this afternoon. Should we switch to cell phones to message? To make it easier to communicate?

The reply with a cell phone number came instantly.

Morgan shut the dating app, picked up his own phone, and called Danielle.

CHAPTER TWENTY EIGHT

The man stared at his phone. Nothing. It had been ten minutes since he'd sent Ivy the number of the burner phone, and she hadn't texted. He went back to the app to see if there were any more messages from her there. He double-checked that he'd given her the right number. He had.

Nothing.

Radio silence.

He took his bat and swung it through the air, tempted to crush the phone with it just like he had with those other women's phones.

But no. He needed it still. Maybe there was an explanation. Ivy got another call or someone came to the door. He'd had her. He could tell. She was interested. She'd call or text soon.

Another five minutes went by with no communication from Ivy on his phone or on the app. He paced the floor, feeling like he was going to jump out of his skin. The anger built more. In his head, he imagined what it would be like when they met. How they'd walk for a while and chat. She'd tell him about her job or her family or some other stupid nonsense. He'd wait until there was no one nearby on the trail or maybe suggest going off the track a bit. She'd probably think he wanted to kiss her. That's what Sandra Cartmill had thought.

As if he would put his mouth against her dirty lying lips.

He'd walk ahead a few steps and then turn. He'd pull his bat from the bag he'd stowed it in, and she'd get that confused look on her face. And then he'd wipe out all expression. His heart beat faster and his mouth went dry thinking about it.

He looked at his phone. Nothing. He checked the computer. Nothing there either. Was she playing some kind of game? Pretending to be hard to get? Stupid bitch. He'd show her.

Then he'd duck into some bushes, change clothes, stroll back out to his car and be gone.

But then what? He could already feel that deflated sensation he'd gotten leaving the arboretum sneaking up on him.

Killing these other women wasn't good enough. Not anymore. Maybe Ivy disappearing was a sign. Maybe it was time. Who needed stupid substitutes like this Ivy person? Maybe it was time to face the woman who had broken his heart for real, not just these stand-ins.

A glance at the calendar reminded him that it was Saturday. She wouldn't be at work. Was she home? Or did she stay out all night? Only way to find out was to go to her apartment and check.

Yes. Yes. He felt his heart rate slow a bit. This felt right. It was time. The buzzing noise in his head went down a few notches in volume.

He grabbed his bat and headed out the door.

CHAPTER TWENTY NINE

"You did what?" Danielle's voice was deceptively mild.

Morgan wasn't fooled. He'd heard her stay absolutely calm when questioning suspects. She wasn't completely happy with him. They could deal with that later. What they needed to do now was use that number to track the killer. "I made a fake profile on HSIPos. I tried to make it as much like Angelica's, Kimberly's, and Sandra's as I could. Someone started messaging me, really pressing to meet up with me today. I've got the number. If he's actively using it, we can track it, right?" Hadn't Divinia said they could use cellular triangulation? Could they do it in real time?

"It's possible," Danielle's agreement sounded slightly grudging.

"Danielle, the guy claimed that I peaked his interest, spelled P-E-A-K, not P-I-Q-U-E. It's the guy. I can feel it."

"You don't know that for sure."

"No, but I think we should check him out." Morgan pressed on anyway. "Should I message him now?"

"No." Danielle's emphatic tone made it clear that there was no discussion on that point. "Come downstairs. I'll pick you up. We'll want to move quickly once we get this guy's location."

Morgan took screenshots of the whole conversation to preserve them. Glad that he was already dressed and ready for the day, he grabbed his wallet, phone, and keys and went downstairs. Danielle arrived five minutes later.

"Do we have a location yet?" he asked as he buckled himself in.

"Not yet, but we should soon." Danielle looked grim.

Disappointment flooded through Morgan. "Can we still find him?"

She looked over at him. "As long as he's using the same burner, we can track him." She hesitated for a second and then said, "That was good work, Morgan. I'm not sure it was smart to do it alone without anyone else from the team, but this might be the final piece we need to catch this guy."

Her phone rang and Danielle hit the button to answer it on the car's speaker. "Yes, Divinia?"

"I'm texting you an address. The burner phone is there and it doesn't appear to be moving."

"Got it." Danielle tapped the address, loaded it into her GPS, and then turned on her lights and siren.

Morgan looked at what she'd programmed in. The address was in the Trinidad neighborhood, right in the triangle that Henry had made on the map. Then he grabbed the handle over his door and hung on. If Morgan had thought Danielle drove fast before, it was because he'd had no idea how fast she could drive.

Danielle killed the lights and siren as they came within a couple of blocks of the location. Pulling up in front of a low-rise apartment building, she screeched to a halt and sprang out of the car.

A woman's scream split the air. Danielle barked into her phone. "I'm going in. Send backup now."

"Help!" Another voice yelled from the side of the building.

Danielle turned to Morgan. "Go check that out. I'll see what's happening inside.."

He watched her race in through the front door of the building. The noise of breaking glass came out of the building, but under the cacophony, Morgan heard moaning.

"Help!" the voice said again.

Morgan raced around the corner to find a man, half in and out of the chokecherry bushes that lined the edge of the building. Curled in a fetal position, he clutched his head. Blood trickled out from between his fingers. He moaned again as Morgan knelt next to him.

"What happened?" Morgan took a quick inventory to see if there were any other injuries. None were immediately apparent.

"Dude clobbered me with a bat!" The man sounded affronted. "All I did was ask him if he knew someone in the building!"

"I'm a doctor. I'd like to check to see if you have a concussion. Would that be okay?"

The man groaned in response.

Morgan quickly checked the man's pupils, lifting each eyelid as gently as he could. They were evenly dilated. That was good. He held up three fingers. "How many fingers am I holding up?"

"Three."

Also good. "Emergency services are on their way. They'll want to take you to the hospital to stitch up that cut, but I think you'll be okay. What did the man look like?"

"Ordinary! Like average everything. White guy. Not too tall. Not too short. Not too thin. Not too fat."

That fit with what they thought they knew about the suspect.

Ordinary enough to fit in pretty much anywhere and everywhere and not excite notice. It absolutely fit with the profile of the man Morgan had been messaging with earlier.

Morgan was about to ask another question when he heard a clanging noise. Looking around the corner of the building, he saw a man running down the fire escape, dragging a baseball bat behind him. He must have jumped out of one of the windows on the back side of the apartments. He was moving fast.

It had to be him, and he was getting away. If he ditched the burner phone and got another one, who knew how many more women might die before they could track him again?

"Stay here," he told the man. "Help is on the way."

Morgan took off around the building in time to see the man run into a parking garage down the street. If he got to his car, would they ever catch him? How many people might suffer before they figured out the man's identity?

Morgan ran faster.

CHAPTER THIRTY

Morgan dashed into the parking garage. The change from the bright sunshine outside to the dimness of the garage momentarily blinded him. He skidded to a stop, trying to hear any clue as to where the man might have gone over the pounding of his heart and the rasping of his own breath.

He heard a clang. What was it? Maybe something hard hitting the metal rails of the stairway to the upper floors? Something like a baseball bat?

Morgan loped to the stairs, taking them two at a time. A smear of blood on the concrete confirming his choice. A door banged up ahead. Morgan rounded the corner and saw the door to the third floor of the garage swing shut.

He was narrowing the gap between them. He could do this. He could get to the murderer before he got away, but not if he hesitated. The question of what he'd do once he caught up with the man flitted through his brain. He had no gun, no cuffs, no training that would allow him to subdue a man with a twist of an arm the way he'd seen Danielle do.

He'd worry about that when he caught the guy. Right now, the most important thing was to keep him from getting away.

Morgan banged into the parking area.

And froze.

Where had the man gone? There was no movement. No sound. Nothing to show Morgan which way to go. He had to be here, though. Morgan crept along the edge of the garage watching for any sign, his eyes still not fully adjusted to the dim light.

Dammit. He could only see this one line of cars if he stayed against the wall. He was going to have to venture farther out into the open. He slipped along using a Ford Expedition as cover.

Still nothing. Maybe he'd lost him. Damn it all to hell.

Morgan took two more steps into the open. The sound of running footsteps behind him alerted him as he turned just in time to duck the swing of the bat.

The man's eyes were wild and staring, almost as if he wasn't seeing

127

Morgan there at all, but someone else. He cocked the bat back again. Morgan stumbled backward and out of the path of the swing. This time the bat struck the Expedition, the blow hard enough to smash a headlight and leave a dent in the hood.

The vehicle's alarm started to ring out, echoing in the dim light of the garage.

The man advanced toward Morgan again. How many times would he be able to duck or swerve? He'd seen what that bat could do and he had no doubt that the man was every bit as enraged at him as he had been at the women he had brutally beaten.

He needed help. He wasn't going to be able to subdue this man by himself. Where was Danielle? Would Danielle hear the car alarm and understand what was happening?

Probably not. Car alarms went off in the city all the time. People barely noticed them.

Maybe multiple car alarms would get her attention, though.

Morgan turned and ran, stopping to kick the grill of a BMW as hard as he could. Its lights began to flash and a siren-like noise joined the beeping of the Expedition.

The kick slowed him down, though, and the man gained on him. Morgan put on a burst of speed and made a quick turn down another parking aisle, this time pounding as hard as he could with his fist on the top of a Lexus's hood, setting its alarm off.

He ducked between the Lexus and a Honda Civic and sprinted down the next aisle, kicking and punching vehicles as he went. The garage echoed with car alarms. Lights flashed everywhere.

Morgan kept running.

CHAPTER THIRTY ONE

Danielle held her side and fought to get her breathing under control. She'd run up the stairs of the apartment building to find one door standing open. She'd thrown it open, announcing herself as FBI.

The man had whirled on her. His bat had already been raised, ready to hit the woman curled into a fetal position on the floor. Danielle hadn't even had a second to brace for the crack to her ribs from the baseball bat.

That, however, had been the last crack he'd gotten in. Danielle had grabbed the bat and spun the man around. He hadn't let go of his weapon, though. Then she shoved forward, using momentum to shove him back into the apartment.

"FBI! Drop the bat! Now!!!" she'd screamed.

The woman on the floor cried out. "Please, Brad. Do what she says! Put the bat down."

His eyes had blazed as he looked between the two women, then he'd taken off, jumping out of the window and onto the fire escape. Clanking noises marking his descent.

"You know him?" Danielle asked the woman.

She nodded, pushing herself up into a sitting position. "His name is Bradley Calvin. We, uh, dated for a while. Then he showed up at my apartment this morning. I didn't even see the bat until he was already inside." Tears streamed down her face. A bruise was blossoming across her cheekbone, and she clutched one arm to her side.

"Do you know where he lives? What he drives?" Danielle asked.

"Y-y-yes." The tears turned into sobs.

Fine. Let the bastard run down the fire escape. He wouldn't get far. She'd have a BOLO out on him and his vehicle in the next five minutes. She grabbed her phone and dialed again. "Make sure you send an ambulance along with the back-up. I have a civilian down." She decided not to mention what she suspected might be a cracked rib. It wasn't like she hadn't dealt with one before and there was damn little the doctors could do about them.

She knelt down next to the woman. "You're going to be okay. More help is on the way."

"Thanks." A confused look came over the woman's face. "But who are you? How did you end up here?"

"My name is Danielle Hernandez. I'm a special agent with the FBI. We were looking for Mr. Calvin." She didn't want to say too much more. This woman would be an important witness when it was time to prosecute Mr. Calvin. "What's your name?"

"Wendy. Wendy Drayton. Thank goodness you got here when you did. I never saw him like that. So angry." She shuddered. "So violent."

The poor woman didn't know the half of it.

In the distance, a car alarm went off. Then another. And another. Danielle frowned. "Is there a parking lot or a garage nearby?"

Wendy nodded. "Just down the alley. Why?"

Danielle wasn't sure, but something was happening and she knew she'd better check it out. She patted Wendy's arm and said, "Help will be here any second now. I need to go see what's happening."

Without waiting for a response, she went out the window that Bradley Calvin had leapt out just a few minutes earlier. Wincing against the pain in her side, she scrambled down the fire escape as fast as she could. Once she was on the ground, she could see the parking garage. It sounded like the alarms of half the cars in the structure were going off.

She ran into the structure. Inside, the noise was deafening. Beeps, honks, and siren noises bounced off the concrete walls, magnifying the wall of sound. Where the hell was it all coming from?

She spun around. Not the first floor. She'd be able to see flashing lights and there was just gray dim light here. She grabbed the door to the stairs and flung it open, not caring how much noise it made as it hit the wall. Then she was pounding up the stairs, each step sending a sharp jolt through her.

On the landing, she pulled her gun and shouldered open the door to the second floor of the garage.

Nothing. No lights. The noise, however, was louder.

With a slight growl in her throat, she ran up to the third floor and did the same thing. She slammed the door open.

This floor was the source of all the noise. Lights flashed everywhere and the noise was deafening.

Ahead of her, she saw Morgan facing off with Bradley Calvin. Calvin had his bat up, ready to strike.

Morgan had nothing, except his wits.

"FBI! Bradley Calvin! Stop and drop the baseball bat! Now!!!" she bellowed.

CHAPTER THIRTY TWO

"Danielle!" She was here! She'd understood his signal.

Morgan skidded to a stop and then turned. The killer still had the bat over his head, ready to smash it down on anything near him.

Danielle had her gun out, still pointed toward the ground. "I don't want to hurt you, Bradley. Put down the bat and put your hands on your head."

"Never!" The man rushed at her, bat swinging wildly.

Despite the way she spun away from him, the bat caught her on her right hand, knocking the gun out of her grip and sending it skittering under a 4Runner. She clutched her hand to her chest.

Morgan ran toward them, knowing all the while that he wouldn't get there in time to keep the man from bashing Danielle's head in.

She stood her ground, seemingly frozen into place. Just as the man got in range of her, she shifted, pivoted on her left foot so that the bat narrowly missed her. Her right foot shot out, catching the man in the stomach.

He doubled over, but only for a second. Then he was back up and swinging again.

Danielle danced back out of his way, dodging him adroitly, but she was favoring one side and holding her hand. She was hurt. How much longer could she keep out of harm's way? He needed to do something. Anything.

"Hey!" Morgan yelled as he came up behind him, wanting to distract him from Danielle.

It worked. The man whirled back toward Morgan. He backpedaled. Now that he had the man's attention, he wasn't sure what to do.

Behind him, he saw Danielle pull out a baton from her belt with her left hand and flick it to its full length. Her chest heaved and she was pale, but she was still in control. She nodded at Morgan and made a rolling gesture with her injured hand, wincing as she did it.

Okay. Keep distracting him. Think. What was this guy's weak spot? His anger. His anger made him act impulsively, violently. Impulsive people made mistakes. That kind of anger came from a deep-seated sense of inadequacy. "That all you got, little man?" Morgan taunted.

The man swung at Morgan again, but Morgan had started getting a sense of how the man moved. He'd studied enough body mechanics to be a quick study in what people could and couldn't do. He ducked and the man missed him, although he heard the whistle of air as the bat passed way too close to his head.

"You can't even swing that bat properly," Morgan said. "How pathetic you are!"

"I. Am. Not. Pathetic!" The man screamed, lifted the bat over his head, and rushed at Morgan.

He wasn't sure how he would duck this time. He wasn't sure which way the man would swing, so he wasn't sure which way to feint. Morgan braced himself for the blow, arms up over his head to protect himself as best as he could, but before the man could bring the bat down on him, Danielle was behind him with her baton fully extended. With one quick movement, she swung it hard at the man's back. He arched back.

For a second, Morgan thought it might not have been enough, that the man was so hopped up on adrenaline and hate that it looked like he'd push right through it. Then the man's knees buckled beneath him, and he went down.

Morgan darted forward and grabbed the bat out of his hand and moved away quickly.

In seconds, Danielle had her knee in the man's back and was cuffing him.

Morgan reached her and doubled over himself, hands braced on his thighs. "Thank you," he gasped out.

"Back at you," she said. "Good distraction moves."

"How's your hand?" he asked.

"I'll live." She looked up at him and grinned. "Nice job of letting me know where you were." Then she turned serious. "But could you maybe stop putting yourself in danger?"

Morgan shook his head and said, "You first."

CHAPTER THIRTY THREE

Morgan clinked his glass against Danielle's. "We did it."

She smiled. "We did." She held her glass higher. "To a great team!"

Henry and Divinia raised their glasses as well.

They were in a small bar near the Federal Triangle, toasting their success in solving what the media had now dubbed the Bat Man Killings. Morgan wasn't crazy about the name, but he appreciated the fact that the media was pointing out how efficiently the FBI had identified and caught the killer, solving everything before widespread panic could spread through the city.

They barely knew the half of it.

"So, explain to me again what this guy was up to?" Henry asked. He'd been part of the team gathering evidence at the parking garage and the apartment building where Bradley Calvin, the man who had called himself Scott Elias on the HSIPos app, had been found instead of part of the team questioning the subject.

Danielle rubbed her uninjured hand over her face and shook her head. "He's delusional. Obviously. We're still putting the details together, but he's been under the treatment of a psychiatrist for years, but opted to go off his meds when he met Wendy Drayton."

Drayton was the woman whose apartment Calvin was in when Danielle confronted him. She'd been beyond shaken by everything that had happened. According to her, she'd broken up with Calvin and that had been that. There'd been a couple of teary phone calls and one time she'd spotted him following her, but she'd had no real contact with him since she'd told him that she wasn't interested in seeing him anymore and then confessed to him why. She'd had no idea that he had become obsessed with her. Morgan's heart had gone out to her when she'd found out that three women had been murdered because of Elias's feelings for her. He'd done all he could to assure her that Elias's psychotic break with reality was not her fault. He wasn't sure she'd believed him.

Danielle continued explaining, "He thought he was in love and that was the only thing he needed to quiet the wild mood swings and violent outbursts he'd been experiencing since he was a teenager." She shook her head, the light catching the bruise on the side of her face that she'd gotten while subduing Aidan Sherrer. "He lost it when she told him that she'd cheated on him, caught HSI, and went completely over the edge when he found out that she was dating men she'd met on HSIPos."

Divinia made a face. "No one wants to be cheated on, but I would think he'd be grateful that she at least didn't give it to him."

"And poor Kimberly!" Henry said. "Wasn't that what happened to her? She got HSI from a boyfriend who cheated on her? Then she ends up being murdered by a guy who dodged getting the disease when the same thing happened to him?"

"Like I said," Danielle continued. "Delusional."

Morgan dropped his head and looked into his drink. He understood how having lost love could derail a person. He hadn't exactly been a model of mental health since Ashley had asked him to move out. He'd drank too much and isolated himself from friends, wallowing in self-pity and recrimination. He was going to have to examine some of his own feelings. Was he obsessing over Ashley? Was it time to truly walk away? Hope still burned in his chest every time he saw her. Hell, it burned every time he heard her voice. Even the passing scent of lavender made him think about her.

"Wait, though," Henry said. "I still don't understand how that leads to him killing people like Kimberly and Angelica and Sandra. They didn't cheat on him."

"The logic is skewed," Morgan said. "When he found out his former lover had met someone else on the HSIPos app, part of him wanted to kill her, but part of him still loved her enough to not want to harm her. He went after women who were similar to her with the assumption that all of them were cheaters like his ex was and that he could work out his anger and hurt by hurting them."

"But where we found him was his actual ex's apartment, right?" Divinia asked.

"It was." Danielle turned her beer in a slow circle on the table. "From what we could get from him, each time he killed one of these other stand-ins for his actual lover, he got less satisfaction from it. He finally got to the point where he was going to kill her. His anger had grown to the point that he wanted to hurt her. His hate was greater than his love."

"So, why was he texting with Morgan earlier in the day?" Henry asked.

"I think he was planning on killing the woman Morgan was pretending to be if he couldn't get to his ex. Apparently he'd been at

135

her apartment the night before and she hadn't been home. His compulsion to kill had gotten stronger and stronger. He was going to kill someone on Saturday. Either his ex or a stand-in for her." Danielle shrugged. "It's never going to make real sense to us. We might be able to understand on some kind of intellectual level the steps he thought were logical, but it's never going to really be something any of us can comprehend."

Henry held up his hands. "Fine by me. I don't want to ever be that crazy."

"Amen," Divinia raised her glass and Henry clinked his to hers.

Danielle was right. They had made a great team. Everyone seemed to bring something different to the group. Morgan hadn't thought before about what their backgrounds were and now he was curious. "So, are you all lawyers and accountants?" he asked.

Divinia nearly did a spit take with her beer. "No! Why do people always think that?" She'd ditched her suit jacket, hanging over the back of her chair and displaying some pretty impressive shoulder and arm muscles.

Henry shook his head. "Not sure. Maybe it was like that in the old days. Now, most of us have criminal justice degrees." He'd also ditched his jacket and loosened his tie. It was the first time Morgan had seen him looking even vaguely rumpled.

Divinia nodded emphatically and raised her hand. "My degree is from Northeastern."

That made sense. There was a hint of a Boston accent there.

"Florida State here," Henry said.

No wonder he never complained about the heat and the humidity.

Morgan turned to Danielle, waiting for her answer. She took another sip of her beer and said nothing.

"Danielle's degree is from John Jay," Henry supplied.

"John Jay?" Morgan was much more familiar with medical schools than with criminal justice colleges.

"John Jay College of Criminal Justice in New York City. Pretty much the créme de la créme of criminal justice programs," Divinia supplied. "Named for the first chief justice of the United States."

Danielle shrugged and raised her glass, "Fierce Advocates for Justice!"

"Cheers to that!" Divinia said and clinked her glass against Danielle's.

"So, law enforcement was always your goal?" Morgan asked.

"An FBI agent is the only thing I've ever wanted to be," Henry said. "I tried to take the most direct route to that goal I could find."

Morgan got that. The only thing he'd ever wanted to be, until a few months ago, was a doctor. Nothing else had ever interested him, except as a path to that goal. Even once he got his medical degree, made it through residency, and passed his boards, he'd never considered any other direction.

He wondered now if that was part of why he felt so empty. Outside of medicine, there really wasn't anything else that left him feeling satisfied and happy.

Until now, of course.

"The Bureau appreciates people from a lot of different backgrounds," Danielle said, giving Morgan a sidelong glance. "Not many agents with medical backgrounds, though."

He took a sip of his beer and then set the glass down. "Is that a hint?"

She turned to look at him face-to-face. "I'm not sure what it is. A hint. A suggestion. Something to think about." She turned her beer around in a circle on the table in front of her again. "You haven't talked a whole lot about that disciplinary hearing. I don't know what you're thinking or feeling about all that, but I do know you have an exceptional natural aptitude for this kind of work. If you were at all interested in pursuing that, I feel like I'd be doing the Bureau a grave disservice by not mentioning it."

Warmth spread outward from his chest from Danielle's words about his aptitude. It meant a great deal to him. He'd spent a lot of time and energy becoming a doctor and establishing a name for himself. Was he willing to walk away from all that? Or would he just be finding a new way to use that knowledge?

He wasn't sure.

"I'll take it under advisement," he said and took another sip of beer. A flash of motion made Morgan sit up straighter. Then he shook his head at himself. Detective Sheehan walked up to the table. Morgan was a little too jumpy. It made sense. It had been a physically exhausting week with too much danger. He forced himself to relax.

"Hi, Danielle," he said and nodded at the rest of the group. He rested his hand on Danielle's shoulder, but gently as if he was aware of her injuries.

"Hi, Brett. Glad you could join us." Danielle smiled up at him.

Morgan exchanged wide-eyed looks with Divinia and Henry. So, he hadn't mistook the vibe between the two of them. Well, good for Danielle. Sheehan seemed like a nice guy who wasn't at all intimidated by Danielle's strength and intelligence. That was probably a rare find.

His heart gave a little pang. He'd always loved how smart Ashley was. It had never made him feel inadequate in any way.

He was getting maudlin. It was time to go home. He finished his beer and stood. "Good night, everyone."

"Will we see you next week?" Divinia asked.

Morgan looked over at Danielle, but she was busy talking to Sheehan. He shrugged and said, "We'll see."

CHAPTER THIRTY FOUR

Morgan let himself back into his apartment.

He stood in the foyer, listening to the quiet. Outside, a car horn blared and someone out on the street laughed loud enough for him to hear it. Inside, the refrigerator hummed. There was no other noise.

He was alone.

The thought reverberated through him and shook him right down to the soles of his shoes. It wasn't just about tonight. He'd been alone for a very long time.

It had been years since his sister had disappeared. His parents' deaths had followed soon after, broken over the loss of their daughter. He'd had no one to count on for years.

In a lot of ways, Ashley had filled that gap for him. She'd been his family, his touchstone. He shouldn't have taken that for granted. He shouldn't have relied on her sweetness and loyalty to keep her at his side. He should have made sure she knew what it all meant to him. Except he wasn't sure that he'd known himself until he didn't have it anymore. Now he had nothing but regrets.

What would his life have been like if Fiona had lived? If she hadn't been snatched away from them before she could come even close to fulfilling her potential? Would he still have thrown himself into his work to the detriment of his marriage? Or would she have helped him stay balanced? Like little sisters all over the world, she'd been more than ready to call him on his bullshit any time of the day or night.

He opened the refrigerator to grab a beer and then thought better of it. He'd already had two at the bar with the team. He didn't need a third.

The team. Maybe he was starting to create a new family. It felt good to be part of these investigations. He'd helped catch two murderers already, and Danielle had been clear that she doubted that they would have been able to do it so quickly without him.

He was, in fact, pretty good at this investigation stuff. Good enough that Danielle thought he should consider training as an actual FBI agent, and he respected the hell out of Danielle. She was damn good at what she did. Could he be that good?

Too bad there hadn't been someone like her on his sister's case. Maybe his family would at least know what had happened to her. It wouldn't make him miss her any less, but at least he could stop wondering.

He started toward his bedroom with a plan to shower and head to bed early. He froze partway there, a thought occurring to him like a flash of lightning. He pulled out his phone and called Danielle.

"Get some rest, Stark," she said. She yawned.

"In a minute." For a second he kicked at the carpet, trying to formulate the question he needed to ask.

"Did you call just to hear my voice?" she asked.

"No. Actually, I called to ask a favor." Now he had to get himself to spit it out. Was he being ridiculous? Could he live with himself if he didn't at least try?

"I think you've earned a favor or two. What can I do for you?"

"Do you think you could get hold of the case files on my sister's disappearance?" Morgan blurted the request out.

There was silence on the other end.

"Danielle?"

"I'm here. I'm thinking."

Morgan would bet money on the fact that her index finger was tapping on something. "What's there to think about?"

She sighed. "Technically, you're a consultant that's hired on a case-by-case basis. We're not working your sister's case. We have no reason to request the files, and we certainly have no reason to show them to you."

Morgan held back a growl. So, now he wasn't part of the "we" who solved cases? What happened to the team? He took a deep breath. He knew she had protocol to follow just as he had had standard operating procedures at the hospital. "It's not like anyone else is working the case, though, right?"

"Right. I, uh, checked on it after you started working with us. It's stone cold. I'm not sure anyone has even accessed the files in several years."

"So we wouldn't be stepping on anyone's toes." It wasn't a question. It was a fact. No one was trying to find out what had happened to Fiona all those years ago. No one ever would unless Morgan did.

"No. We wouldn't be stepping on toes." She sounded reluctant to agree.

It didn't escape him that she was back to using "we," though. They

140

were back to being a team. "Where's the harm, Danielle? Maybe, just maybe, it would give me some closure too. I'd be able to understand what was done and why and what might have happened. At the time, we were all so distraught, I don't think my family registered much of what was going on and I certainly didn't have any context to put the information in." And context was key to almost everything. Granted, he'd only worked on two investigations, but he'd learned so much already.

"Okay. Okay. I see your point." She sighed again. "You've done me plenty of favors in the past few weeks too. I owe you at least one."

"Thank you," he said. "Thank you so much. I really appreciate it."

"Don't get too excited. I haven't done it yet. Let me make some calls and figure out what's where. I'll get back to you. If it's all digitized, I might be able to access it fairly quickly."

His heart lifted. "Great. Talk to you soon."

"You know it." She hung up.

Morgan stripped off his sweaty clothes and dumped them into the laundry hamper in the corner of his bedroom, then stood under the stinging spray of the shower until it ran cold. He heard the buzz of an email alert on his phone as he wrapped a towel around his waist.

He forced himself to get dressed, sliding into a pair of sweats and an old Emory University t-shirt before looking to see if the email was from Danielle. It was.

She'd written: I hope this helps you with that whole closure thing.

He smiled. That was so her. Attached were five separate files. The first file was the case notes. Morgan read through the description of what had happened to his family with a strange sense of remove.

He hadn't been there the evening his sister hadn't come home. He'd already been in college. Here on the page was a transcription of his mother's frantic call to the local police, arguing hard that her daughter wasn't the kind of girl to run away or forget to let her parents know where she was going, pressing them to start looking for her right away instead of waiting to see if she'd turn up. They'd still made her wait until the next morning. If they had acted quicker, would the outcome have been different? Morgan rubbed the back of his neck, trying to stay calm as he read.

Then there was the rundown of what the police had done, going over some of the ground his parents had already covered. Calling her friends. Checking at the school.

When Fiona still hadn't come home by the morning after that, the search had started for real. Volunteers had been organized to search.

Morgan had been home by that time. He'd gone out with the search parties, walking side-by-side through the countryside around their home, calling her name, looking for signs of her, and coming home each night demoralized and increasingly desperate.

Then they'd brought in the search dogs. He remembered the way his mother had turned to his father, burying her face in his chest. Afraid of what they might find. It had ended up being the one and only break they'd had in the entire case.

The dogs had found Fiona's backpack. It had been tossed up high in a tree, deliberately hidden from view, as if someone knew the searchers would all be looking at the ground.

From there the trail had gone cold.

Morgan opened the next file. This one held photos. There was a photo of Fiona, of course. A candid photo of the last vacation their family had taken at Cape Cod. The ocean air had tossed her dark hair. Her head was tilted back and she was laughing. He traced the outline of her face on the computer screen.

He hadn't seen that photo in forever, but now that he had, it came rushing back. The sound of her laugh. The twinkle in her eye when she would tease him. The way she twirled one lock of her hair around her index finger when she was working on a hard math problem. Her absolute inability to cook anything without burning it, including a very memorable mac and cheese dinner.

His chest tightened and his eyes burned with unshed tears. He pushed on, though.

Next there was a photo of the backpack, then of each and every item that had been inside it. All the stuff you'd expect to find in a teenager's backpack. A three-ring binder with dividers for each of her classes. A couple of folders for hand-outs. A brush. Lip gloss. It was the fifth photo of those that froze him in place.

He stared down at the photo. Could he be seeing things? He grabbed a small magnifier that he used for medical texts with tiny footnotes and placed it over the photo.

He wasn't imagining things.

Morgan sat back in his chair, not quite sure he believed what had just happened.

Had he really found the first lead to solving his sister's disappearance that they'd had in more than a decade?

NOW AVAILABLE!

TOO FAR GONE
(A Morgan Stark FBI Suspense Thriller—Book 3)

When victims of a serial killer are found dead by injection of a new pharmaceutical, Morgan Stark, a brilliant doctor-turned FBI agent, is summoned. With an abundance of theories as to the motive and murder, Morgan may be the only one who can wade through the medical possibilities to enter this killer's mind. But will he be too late?

"A brilliant book. I couldn't put it down and I never guessed who the murderer was!"
—Reader review for Only Murder

TOO FAR GONE is book #3 in a new series by #1 bestselling and critically acclaimed mystery and suspense author Rylie Dark, which begins with TOO LATE (book #1).

Morgan Stark is a renowned surgeon, acclaimed by his colleagues for his brilliance as a diagnostician. But when his close friend and protégé resident is murdered, Morgan feels compelled to help the FBI decipher the trail of medical clues and bring the killer to justice.

FBI Special Agent Quinn Carter, 28, a rising star in the BAU, equally esteemed by her colleagues for her brilliance and determination, is not used to turning to a doctor for help in solving crimes. This unlikely partnership, though, may just surprise them both.

Morgan and Quinn grapple with the motive behind this erratic killer. Why use a drug that saves people to kill them? Might the killer himself be sick? Could rival pharmaceutical companies be involved?

But Morgan and Quinn feel the motive is more primal.

And that this killer, if not stopped, will soon strike again.

A cat-and-mouse thriller with harrowing twists and turns and filled with heart-pounding suspense, the MORGAN STARK mystery series offers a fresh twist on the genre as it introduces two brilliant protagonists who will make you fall in love and keep you turning pages late into the night.

Future books in the series will be available soon.

"I loved this thriller, read it in one sitting. Lots of twists and turns and I didn't guess the
culprit at all... Already pre-ordered the second!"
—Reader review for Only Murder

"This book takes off with a bang... An excellent read, and I'm looking forward to the next book!"
—Reader review for SEE HER RUN

"Fantastic book! It was hard to put down. I can't wait to see what happens next!"
—Reader review for SEE HER RUN

"The twists and turns kept coming. Can't wait to read the next book!"
—Reader review for SEE HER RUN

"A must-read if you enjoy action-packed stories with good plots!"
—Reader review for SEE HER RUN

"I really like this author and this series starts with a bang. It will keep you turning the pages till the end of the book and wanting more."
—Reader review for SEE HER RUN

"I can't say enough about this author! How about 'out of this world'! This author is going to go far!"
—Reader review for ONLY MURDER

"I really enjoyed this book... The characters were alive, and the twists and turns were great. It will keep you reading till the end and leave you wanting more."
—Reader review for NO WAY OUT

Rylie Dark

Bestselling author Rylie Dark is author of the SADIE PRICE FBI SUSPENSE THRILLER series, comprising six books (and counting); the MIA NORTH FBI SUSPENSE THRILLER series, comprising six books (and counting); the CARLY SEE FBI SUSPENSE THRILLER, comprising six books (and counting); and the MORGAN STARK FBI SUSPENSE THRILLER, comprising three books (and counting).

An avid reader and lifelong fan of the mystery and thriller genres, Rylie loves to hear from you, so please feel free to visit www.ryliedark.com to learn more and stay in touch.

Lightning Source UK Ltd.
Milton Keynes UK
UKHW012043090223
416722UK00003B/233